Harlequin Romance®

presents

international bestselling author

BARBARA HANNAY

Her Secret, His Son won the *CataRomance* Reviewer's
Choice Award 2004:

"Barbara Hannay has produced an emotional
rollercoaster of a novel that packs a heavy punch.
Her Secret, His Son reduced me to tears and I loved it.
The novel is chock full of emotions and heart-warming
characters. The author has used an entertaining blend
of American and Australian settings to produce a lush
novel that anyone would want to visit…. This book is
a pure gem that has a charm and an emotional depth
that shines through to the reader. Do not miss this
very special book that will take you on an unforgettable
journey. Barbara Hannay: *Her Secret, His Son* a truly
magical ride."
—Kelly Bowerman, *CataRomance*

Dear Reader,

Sometimes when I'm in the middle of writing a book I realize I'm tapping into something bigger than I expected. I uncover characters and issues and emotions that seem to have a power of their own.

I felt this happen when I was writing *Her Secret, His Son*. This book is a little different from my Outback stories in that it is mostly set in Washington, D.C., and Virginia. The hero, Tom Pirelli, is an Australian SAS soldier, fighting in an elite antiterrorist unit with Ed McBride, a U.S. Army Ranger.

I should mention that I haven't tried to justify war. This book is 100 percent romance—deeply emotional romance. My heroine, Mary, has terrible choices to make. But her story is played out against a background of contemporary strife.

The city of Townsville, where I live, has a large military base and our links with the U.S. forces go back to World War II. *Her Secret, His Son* is my small tribute to the huge sacrifices made by our military people and their loved ones now and in the past.

Lastly, this story finishes in one of my favorite places in the world—the beautiful Atherton Tablelands of north Queensland—where I am now spending more time in our little cottage, tucked away on a misty green hillside.

Warmest wishes,

Barbara Hannay

HER SECRET,
HIS SON

Barbara Hannay

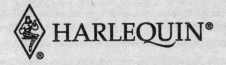

TORONTO • NEW YORK • LONDON
AMSTERDAM • PARIS • SYDNEY • HAMBURG
STOCKHOLM • ATHENS • TOKYO • MILAN • MADRID
PRAGUE • WARSAW • BUDAPEST • AUCKLAND

ISBN 0-373-03886-0

HER SECRET, HIS SON

First North American Publication 2006.

Copyright © 2004 by Barbara Hannay.

Barbara Hannay was born in Sydney, educated in Brisbane and has spent most of her adult life living in tropical north Queensland, where she and her husband have raised four children. While she has enjoyed many happy times camping and canoeing in the bush, she also delights in an urban lifestyle—chamber music, contemporary dance, movies and dining out. An English teacher, she has always loved writing, and now, by having her stories published, she is living her most cherished fantasy. Visit www.barbarahannay.com

Barbara Hannay on her inspiration for *Her Secret, His Son:*

"In 2003 I had the privilege of spending a week as the houseguest of a top-ranking U.S. general and I was taken on a private tour of the Pentagon. This visit and the sights of Washington, D.C., Arlington and the Lincoln Memorial were wonderful inspirations for this book."

Books by Barbara Hannay

CHAPTER ONE

AT TEN minutes before midnight Mary Cameron crept out of bed, fully clothed, her heart racing. Thick carpet silenced her movements as she tiptoed to the window, drew the curtain aside and peered through the slanted slats of the venetian blinds.

Tom was waiting for her.

He was standing on the corner, just outside the pale lemon circle cast by the street light. She could see the defiant splash of his white T-shirt beneath the bulkiness of his black leather jacket. His wide shoulders were squared and his hands rested lightly on his hips, as if he were poised ready for action.

Truth was, Tom Pirelli was *always* ready for action. And, on this balmy North Queensland winter's night, he was ready to run away with her.

A delicious thrill rippled through her. With one finger she dipped a slat in the blind so she could see Tom more clearly and he lifted his hand to wave. His mouth tilted in his familiar unhurried smile and her heart flipped. By this time tomorrow they would be far away from Townsville.

And she would be Tom Pirelli's *wife*.

Over the past weeks she had thought of nothing but marrying Tom. She hadn't been able to concentrate on her studies, had hardly heard any of her family's conversations. The single most important thing in her life was a twenty-two-year-old soldier with a devastating slow smile and even more devastating, slow kisses.

He filled her head and her heart and she was certain she couldn't possibly live without him.

'I'm coming, Tom,' she whispered as she released the slat and let the curtain drop back into place.

Heart knocking in her chest, she stooped to pick up her small backpack. It held little more than a change of clothes and her toiletries, but she couldn't risk carrying a bulky pack through the dark house. It would be a disaster if she knocked something over and woke her parents. Besides, she would be travelling on the back of Tom's motorbike, which meant travelling light.

Travelling light and lighthearted and in love.

With Tom.

Her insides jumped and danced with excitement. She was so heart-and-soul in love with Tom that it still came as a shock that he loved her back. She had to be the luckiest girl in Australia. No, make that the universe.

Without a backward glance at the pretty bedroom that had been home to her secret dreams for so many years, she hurried out into the hallway.

Here, there was danger.

The polished timber floors of the living areas were noisy, so she carried her shoes in her hands and prayed that her socks would muffle her footsteps. All would be lost if her father woke up.

Oh, help! At the thought of her father, Mary came to an abrupt halt, frozen by a panicky rush of guilt. Heaven knew this wasn't the way she wanted to be married. Until she'd met Tom she'd enjoyed a happy relationship with her parents, and it was just awful now to be torn between her family ties and her passion for her man.

But her father wouldn't listen when she tried to defend Tom, so he'd left her with absolutely no choice. She could only hope that once she and Tom were married all would be well. Her father would *have* to see that they were meant for each other.

She had no doubt that she and Tom would win her parents around. Once her dad got to know Tom, he couldn't help but admire him. Tom would be an adoring husband. In the years to come he'd be a wonderful father for their children and the perfect son-in-law for her parents. Everything would be fine just as soon as she was safely outside. With Tom.

She took a deep breath and began to tiptoe forward again.

She'd practised creeping through the midnight-silent house several times in the past weeks, so she knew about the creaking board outside her parents' bedroom and another near the entrance to the dining room. Once these were safely bypassed she began to breathe more easily.

As she neared the front of the house she could hear the hum of the dishwasher in the kitchen. It was reaching the end of its long cycle. Brilliant timing! She could co-ordinate the moment she opened the front door with the final gush of the rinse water gurgling down the drain.

At last she was safely through the house and in the slate-tiled front entry, where faint light from the street filtered through long narrow panels of glass on either side of the front door. Almost free.

The hiss of water in the kitchen was her signal. Quickly, Mary thrust her feet into her shoes, took a deep breath and stepped to the door, then slowly, slowly, turned the handle of the doorknob, praying that it wouldn't make a sound. Not now. Not with freedom so near.

Not with Tom waiting outside.

Already she could picture the glimmer in his dark eyes when she reached him, the way he would haul her close, enfolding her inside the protection of his leather jacket. Already she could feel the warmth of his arms around her and his lips nuzzling the side of her neck as he whispered, 'Mary-Mary.'

Holding her breath, Mary inched the door open and the potted palm beside her seemed to move. It startled her and she jerked the door back, making its hinges squeak.

'What the hell do you think you're doing?'

Her father's voice exploded beside her in the dark.

Swift and terrible as a lightning strike, panic flashed through her. With a gasp of despair, she wrenched the door wide and hurled herself forward, but hands, strong as talons, gripped her.

'No!' she cried as she struggled to tug herself free. 'You can't stop me!'

Her arm was almost pulled from its socket and her backpack fell to the floor as her father hauled her back through the doorway.

'No,' she sobbed. 'You can't do this! Please, no, you don't understand.'

She cried out as the door slammed shut. Horrified, she slipped sideways out of her father's grasp and took off through the dark kitchen, skirting the island bench as she headed for the back door.

'Don't be so stupid, girl,' her father roared, hot in pursuit. Again his hands came from behind her and he seized her arm. Again she tried to break free, but he was too big and too strong. She had no hope of trying to outrun a trained army officer in his own home. She was yanked backwards and pushed hard against the slats of the louvred door on the pantry cupboard.

'You've got to let me go,' she panted. 'I'm an adult. I have every right.'

Colonel Cameron's dark face loomed above her. 'Call yourself an adult?' he sneered. 'An adult wouldn't slink away in the middle of the night to a pick up with a no-good lout like Pirelli.'

'He's not a lout. You don't know him.'

Light flooded the kitchen and, through her pain and her tears, Mary squinted against the sharp brightness. She saw her mother standing in the doorway in her nightgown and, behind her, her cousin Sonia, staring with huge, fascinated eyes.

'You can't hold me prisoner,' Mary sobbed at them. 'I'm not going to let you spoil this. I have to go. Let me go!'

'Mary, be reasonable,' came her mother's voice.

'No! *You* be reasonable,' Mary cried back, as she struggled against her father's tight hold.

Refusing to look at his angry red face, she focused on her mother, who looked so much more vulnerable at midnight in her pale nightgown and without the careful mask of the make-up she always wore.

'You're backing Dad against Tom when you don't even know him. You won't let me bring Tom into our house, but you can't do this to me. I'm twenty, Mum. I'm old enough to know what I want. Tom and I love each other and you've got to let me live my life. I've got to go to him. I've got to!'

'Over my dead body,' her father roared and, to emphasise his point, he gripped her shoulders harder and forced her back against the cupboard again.

'Ralph, there's no need to be rough,' came her mother's voice.

Mary moaned and tears streamed down her cheeks. Tears of rage, not pain. Tom was waiting on the foot-path. What had he heard? What had he thought when the kitchen lights came on? What would he do if she didn't show up?

Would she ever be able to see him again? She *had* to. No one could possibly understand how desperately she needed him. Every cell in her body yearned for the re-assurance of his strong arms around her. She needed him to hold her as he murmured his pet name for her, over and over—the way he did when they made love. 'Mary-Mary, Mary-Mary.'

Her father's vicelike grip loosened a fraction, but not enough to release her. 'Stop snivelling, girl,' he hissed. 'I can't believe my own daughter could be such a fool. When you come to your senses you'll be grateful. You'll thank me for this.'

'Never!' Mary cried, hating him. She couldn't bear to look at him and she let her tears fall, making no attempt to stop the sobs that racked her. 'You've d-decided you don't like T-Tom simply because he's not an officer and—and he rides a motorbike.'

Her father swore and gave her shoulders a shake. 'Pirelli is a hooligan, Mary. You know he's been up before the Provost marshal for speeding, and he was in-volved in a brawl at a local nightclub. I'm not letting a man like that touch my daughter.'

'But he has!' Mary cried with a surge of triumphant defiance, and she lifted her head to meet her father's hard grey glare.

I live for Tom Pirelli's touch.

'Where is he? I'll kill him!'

'Ralph, for heaven's sake,' her mother interrupted, coming close enough to tap her husband's elbow in a hesitant attempt to soothe him. 'It's the middle of the night. Keep your voice down. Why don't we go into the lounge and sit down and talk this through sensibly?'

'There's nothing to talk through,' Mary protested. 'Can't you both understand? I truly love Tom and he loves me. I can't live without him. If you don't let me go, you'll have ruined my life.'

'Consider it ruined,' her father snapped.

Mary wept noisily. How could her parents be so unjust and cruel to their own daughter? She felt as if they'd hurled her into the ocean with rocks tied to her feet. Inconsolable, she slumped against the pantry door. Her father released his pressure, but she knew it was useless to try to escape. She let her spine bump down the louvred slats as she slid to the floor and crouched in a miserable, undignified huddle with her arms wrapped around her bent knees.

She wanted to die.

Her cousin Sonia's voice reached her through her misery. 'Would you like me to go and tell Tom that you're not coming?'

Mary's head snapped up.

Sonia stepped closer and Mary realised for the first time that she was fully dressed, as was her father. Had they known her plans?

Her cousin had been living with her family for the past year because she was studying law at James Cook University. Mary drove Sonia to university each day but, because they were in different faculties, they saw little of each other on campus.

They hadn't become close, and now the bright, fascinated light in Sonia's eyes bothered Mary. But she couldn't leave Tom stranded on the footpath waiting.

'He's waiting on the corner. Go and tell him what's happened. Tell him that I'll work something out,' she said.

'Don't bother yourself, Sonia,' interjected her father.

'If anyone talks to Private Pirelli tonight, it will be me. I'd talk to the mongrel with my fists except that I don't fancy being court-martialled for assault.'

Her mother had switched the kettle on and now it came to the boil. She turned to pour bubbling hot water into mugs with tea bags.

From behind Colonel Cameron's back, Sonia sent Mary what might have been a sympathetic smile if her eyes hadn't gleamed with suppressed excitement. 'I'll go back to bed, then,' she mumbled sleepily, but then she sent Mary a wink. And, as Mary watched Sonia shuffle out of the room, she knew her cousin planned to sneak out through the back of the house to find Tom.

She wished she found that thought more comforting.

'How did you know?' she asked her parents, suddenly suspicious. 'You were waiting up for me.'

'Some people claim that Army Intelligence is an oxy-moron, but it comes in handy,' her father drawled, and his mouth curved into a smug half-smile.

Still huddled on the floor, Mary shot him a glare filled with venom.

He let out an impatient sigh. 'Look, Mary, I'm quite prepared to tell you why I'm opposing this. I simply don't trust Pirelli.'

'You haven't given him a chance.'

'I'm not going to. I can't afford to take risks when my only daughter is involved. I don't trust a guy who just doesn't add up.'

'What do you mean?'

'Well…he tops bloody everything. IQ tests; language tests; shooting competitions.'

'Really? He never told me that. But how can that be bad?'

A brief, startled reaction flickered in her father's eyes,

but he quickly recovered. 'There's something wrong with a guy who's as bright as that and still acts like a hooligan. It's not just his behaviour around town. On exercises, we never know what Pirelli will do. He questions and challenges commands. He won't conform. That's why I knocked back his promotion.'

'Did you really?' she murmured. 'He didn't tell me that either.'

'No, he wouldn't, would he?' Her father's jaw shot forward like a bulldog's. 'Private Pirelli is a bad bet, Mary. He's the kind of soldier who will want to play heroes. He'll throw himself into the front line. You know what I'm saying, don't you?'

'You mean he's courageous.'

'I mean he's a fool. And tonight he's proved it if he thinks I can't see what he's planning.'

Mary's insides turned hollow.

'Ralph,' said her mother in a warning tone. 'Be careful.'

'I'm not the one who has to be careful, Anne. It's Mary.' He crouched low beside Mary and placed a broad hand on her shoulder. 'Pirelli's plan was to have his way with my daughter—to play with her and then leave.'

'No!' His words winded her. She couldn't breathe.

'It's the truth, Mary. This crazy pretence at elopement is payback.'

'No!' Struggling for breath, she felt smothered by a thick black fog. Heavy, suffocating clouds crushed her chest as she tried to stand. She clutched at the pantry doorknob, trying to gain leverage, to regain her dignity. To fight back. 'No, you're wrong. It's not like that. Tom loves me. He wants to marry me.'

'Grow up, Mary. Do you really think there's going to be a wedding? Wake up, girl. Marriage is the last thing on Private Pirelli's mind. Did he tell you he's put in for a transfer to Perth, on the other side of Australia?'

'No, no-o-o!' Her protest edged into a scream.

'You'd better believe it, honey.' Her father's unexpectedly gentle voice reached her through the fog. 'I'm sorry, but the little adventure he had planned for tonight was all about payback because he missed a promotion. Don't you see? Tom Pirelli has been using you, sweetheart.'

CHAPTER TWO

THE soft red glow of a night vision light filled the Sea Knight helicopter's cabin. Dressed in camouflage gear and floppy bush hats, the six members of the elite joint forces anti-terrorist squad sat alert and ready.

'Five minutes out,' came the crackling message from the pilot through their headphones.

Tom Pirelli checked his equipment one more time. Everything was ready. His gear was strapped down and the J-hook on his automatic weapon was secured so that it couldn't pop loose or hook him up when the team made their fast rope descent to the drop zone in the South-East Asian jungle below.

There was nothing to do now but wait, and for a luxurious moment, he allowed his thoughts to turn away from the grim task ahead to a picture of his home—his family's tea plantation on a sleepy green hillside, high on the Atherton Tableland in Far North Queensland.

He'd been thinking about home a lot lately. The morning mists, the welcoming smells of baking in his mother's kitchen in winter and, in summer, the lacy splendour of tropical ferns in his nonna's greenhouse.

It was a long time—too damn long—since he'd seen his family. But, since he'd joined the Australian Special Air Services, he'd been posted to so many foreign hot spots and had been home so rarely he'd almost forgotten how much he loved the old place. Yeah, it had definitely been too long.

A rap on his shoulder snapped him back to the present. Ed McBride, one of the US Rangers who'd teamed with the SAS for this joint forces mission, was leaning towards him.

'Can you do me a favour, man?' Ed shouted above the whining engines and the roar of the rotors.

'What kind of favour?' Tom's eyes narrowed as he tried to read Ed's expression—not easy given that his face was blackened in readiness for the night's task.

'Take this.' Ed thrust a watch into Tom's hand—not a high-tech serviceman's watch, but a gold civilian job— an old-fashioned one at that. The kind that accompanied the golden handshake when old codgers retired. 'Can you stick it in your pocket and look after it for me?'

'You don't need me to look after your stuff.'

'Come on, man. Just this once. In case anything happens to me.'

Tom frowned. 'Don't talk rubbish, mate. This mission's going to be a piece of cake.'

'I know, I know, but just humour me on this and take the damn watch.'

Turning the watch over, Tom saw that the back was engraved and he used his penlight to read the inscription. *To Robert Edward McBride. In appreciation. January 10, 1925.*

'It was my great-grandfather's watch,' Ed yelled. 'It's been handed down through the family. My dad passed it on to me and I want to keep it safe for my boy.'

'For your son?'

'Yeah.'

The team didn't talk too much about their families— it was if talking about home might soften them somehow, and in this deadly game they couldn't afford any kind of distraction. But Tom knew Ed had a wife and son back in Virginia. He'd seen a photo of the little fellow. The boy had been wearing his father's cap and his face was in shadow, but he'd gained the impression that the youngster was sturdy and cute with a cheeky grin.

He shoved the watch back into Ed's hand. 'You keep this for your kid. It'll be perfectly safe with you.'

'No!'

The urgency in Ed's voice sent a chill spiking down Tom's spine.

'Do it for me,' Ed pleaded. 'Just this once.'

'Don't talk crap,' Tom shouted angrily. What was eating Ed? Special Operatives never lost their cool. Never showed fear. Or doubt.

But deep down he knew what Ed was trying to say. It was a feeling a soldier could get—a premonition that something was going to go wrong.

'Please, Tom,' Ed insisted. 'I thought we were buddies.'

'Well, yeah, of course we are. We're more than buddies. We're mates.'

It was true. He genuinely liked this American with his constant smile, spiky blond crewcut and marine-blue eyes. Ed was a crack soldier and an all-round great guy. Easygoing, salt of the earth, apple pie and Fourth of July all rolled into one six-foot, muscle-bound package. A walking-talking-fighting Good Guy.

Tom hadn't expected to become close friends with the American, but he and Ed had formed a unique bond. They respected each other. Without question they trusted each other's considerable battle skills, and they shared a similar outlook as well as a similar string of military decorations. But beyond that they shared something more important—a sense of humour that had helped them in the grimmer moments.

Until now.

Tom looked again at the gold watch. There was nothing particularly fancy about it. Its value could only be sentimental. And this was *not* a time for sentiment.

'One minute out.'

The signal was given for the team to unbuckle their seat belts and move to the ramp at the rear of the chopper.

Their craft dropped to a hover and the men stood, bracing themselves. Ed would be the fifth man to descend the fast rope, while Tom, who was the squad's leader, would bring up the rear.

'Please!' Ed yelled once more, holding the watch out to Tom.

Already, the assigned soldier was shoving the coiled rope off the ramp and leaning out as he watched it fall to the ground. Then he signalled to Zeke, the first man to descend. Zeke grabbed the rope with both hands, hooked it with one foot, pivoted, jumped clear of the ramp and disappeared, sliding down.

Tom sighed. 'OK, give it here,' he said, taking the watch from Ed and zipping it quickly into an inner pocket. 'But I'll be giving this bloody thing straight back to you just as soon as this mission is over.'

He lowered his night goggles and Ed's teeth flashed green as he grinned.

'Thanks, bud,' he called back to Tom. Then, still grinning, he turned, ready to descend.

CHAPTER THREE

IT WAS a warm summer's day in Virginia but Ethan had the beginnings of a cold.

Mary frowned as she reached over the breakfast table to lay a hand on her son's forehead. He'd started coughing during the night and this morning his nose was snuffly and his skin slightly warm. If he had a raised temperature she would have to keep him home from school today.

'Is your throat sore?' she asked, noting the way he dawdled his spoon around and around his bowl of cereal, then sipped half-heartedly at his orange juice.

Ethan nodded, and beneath his floppy blond fringe his big brown eyes grew round as he sent her his sad puppy look.

She'd seen rather too much of that look lately.

'Why didn't Dad come home for Fourth of July?' he asked her. 'He promised.'

Mary sighed. Ever since she'd received the terrible news that her husband was missing in action and presumed dead, she'd tried to keep the news from Ethan. Coping with her own sickening fear was hard enough.

Ethan idolised Ed, and Mary was concerned that his cold was a symptom of his distress as much as a seasonal chill.

'Sometimes soldiers can't keep their promises, but I'm hoping Daddy will be home very soon, sweetheart.'

She wasn't prepared to tell him the truth. She still clung to the hope that Ed was safe and well.

But the boy was supersensitive to her tension, to her friends' kid glove treatment of them both, to Grandma McBride's open concern and Grandpa McBride's stoic acceptance.

Not knowing was the worst. There was so little news—just that Ed was missing behind enemy lines. She couldn't stop thinking about what might have happened to him. As an Army wife, she'd always known something like this might happen, particularly when he'd joined the Special Squad, but she'd pushed that knowledge to the back of her mind.

But now he was *missing*. And missing could mean so many things. Awful, unbearable things.

'What's the matter, Mummy?'

Oh, God, she'd nearly given in to tears in front of Ethan. Flashing him a quick, tight smile, she said, 'Would you like to stay home from school and rest up today?'

He nodded listlessly. 'Can I watch TV?'

'Sure,' she said, frowning as she watched him wander through to the adjoining family room.

Until they'd received the news about Ed, Ethan had always loved school. She told herself that one day wouldn't hurt. Perhaps today, when he wasn't well, the comforting sight of the familiar bright puppets on his favourite children's show would cheer him up.

As her son settled on to a beanbag, in front of the television, she poured herself another cup of coffee, put her feet up on the opposite chair and forced her thoughts to practical things—like the changes she would have to make to her day's plans.

With Ethan sick, she wouldn't be able to play tennis this morning but, because she ran her business from home, she would still be able to get on with her work this afternoon. She reached to the phone on the nearby kitchen counter, planning to call one of her tennis friends, but she'd only dialled the first digit when the doorbell rang.

Surprised, she swung her feet from the chair and looked around for her slip-on shoes. Where had she left them? Her hand flew to her hair. She hadn't taken any trouble when she'd brushed it this morning and she hadn't given a thought to make-up. Who would be calling her at this hour? It was too early for tennis.

Could it be someone from the Army?

Oh, God. The unwelcome thought hit her like a smack in the face. The Army would send someone around if there was bad news about Ed.

Her stomach screwed itself into a nervous knot as her feet found shoes beneath the table. *Ed, please be safe. Please let him be safe.*

Her hand was shaking as she opened the front door.

'Good morning, Mrs McBride—'

Oh, help!

In an instant she recognised the man standing on her doorstep.

Tom.

Tom Pirelli… Staring at her as if he'd seen a ghost.

After eight long years.

'Mary!'

Tom. She couldn't get a word out. She couldn't speak, couldn't think, couldn't *breathe*. Her hands pressed against her chest as she felt something snag in its centre, as if a pulled thread was unravelling her heart, spooling her back into the past.

Within a mad second she was twenty again, feeling the same swift clutch in her throat, the same painful, aching rush she'd always felt whenever she saw Tom.

Her legs trembled. She was drenched in a thousand sweet memories.

Eight years had hardly changed him. He was dressed in neat civilian trousers and a snowy white open-necked shirt, but his black hair was still clipped short, military style.

Perhaps he was more mature-looking—his body more honed and muscular, his face a little more rugged, lined and lean—but in every other way he was the same Tom. His eyes were the same haunting, deep black-brown and were teamed with the same strongly defined cheekbones and, heaven help her, the same mouth.

But today there was no slow smile. Tom Pirelli looked as shell-shocked as she felt.

'It's you. It's Mary Cameron.'

'Yes. I— I'm M-Mary McBride now.'

'*McBride?*' He seemed to wince as he bit off an exclamation. 'You don't mean—don't tell me you're Ed's *wife.*'

He looked so suddenly ill her heart almost stopped beating. She opened her mouth to ask him how on earth he was connected with Ed, but confusion and fear held her back.

'Yes,' she said. 'I'm Ed McBride's wife.'

'Oh, God, Mary. I can't believe this. I— I—' He shook his head and rubbed the back of his hand over his brow. 'I had no idea you were still here in America.'

She was so numb she couldn't think of the right way to respond.

'I hadn't heard you were married,' Tom went on. 'I heard that your father was posted back to Australia and I assumed—'

'No, I didn't go back with my parents.'

Tom muttered something harsh beneath his breath and

Mary felt her face heat. Seeing him sent her compass points suddenly haywire, her emotions swinging wildly between joy and despair. She had loved this man. She'd broken her heart over Tom Pirelli and it had taken far too long to mend.

But this was the very worst time to be meeting him again. If she'd had Ed by her side, she would have been able to handle this. But alone?

'Why are you here?' she managed to ask.

At first he shook his head, as if he couldn't remember, then blinked and said, 'Uh—because of Ed. We were in the same Special Squad.'

'Really?' His words sank in. 'You mean you've found him? No one told me. Is he OK?'

'No, Mary. I'm sorry if I misled you. Ed hasn't been found.'

'Oh.' She swayed against the door frame and her eyes closed as tears burned against the insides of her eyelids and stung her throat. The combined shock of seeing Tom on top of her worries about Ed were too much to take in. Covering her mouth with her hand, she tried to hold her emotions in check, but beneath her fingers her lips twisted as she struggled not to cry.

Tom's throat worked. His dark eyes shimmered as he said, 'Please accept my sympathy, Mary. Ed was—the best.'

'Don't say that. You make it sound like he's dead.'

He frowned. 'But—'

She shook her head. 'He's only missing. I haven't given up hope. I'm sure he'll be found, that he'll come back.'

'Yes, of course. I understand.' Tom's eyes avoided hers and his tone implied that he understood her words but didn't quite agree with her.

There was an awkward pause while he stood on her doorstep and she stood with her hand on the door, knowing that if he were any other man she would invite him inside. But inviting Tom into her home seemed impossible. It felt too momentous, too meaningful.

'What about you, Tom? Are you married?'

'No.'

The single syllable seemed to hang in the warm July air the way the boom of a brass gong lingers.

Mary groped for another question. 'So... What have you been doing?'

His mouth twisted into a bitter smile. 'Same as your husband—defending the free world.' For a moment he studied her with hard, dark eyes. 'I have something for your son,' he said. 'Ed wanted me to bring it to him.'

At the mention of Ethan, Mary felt a fresh surge of dismay. Her stomach churned. Their gazes locked and her cheeks burned as years of silence and buried emotions hung in the air between them. So many unanswered questions...

After all this time... What was Tom thinking? What was he feeling? What did he expect from her?

She turned back and could see through the house to the family room. Ethan was lying upside-down on the beanbag, laughing at the antics on the television screen. Already he looked much brighter than he had at breakfast.

'Ethan's home from school today,' she told Tom. 'He has a cold.'

'Would it be better if I waited till he's feeling better?'

Goodness, that would mean seeing Tom again. Was that wise? 'How long will you be here?'

'Just a few days.'

'Well, I don't want to mess you around. I'm sure you

have lots of other things you want to do. And if you've brought Ethan a gift from his father it might cheer him up.'

'It's a watch.' Tom patted his pocket.

'A watch?'

'I believe it's the McBride family watch.'

'Oh, no!' Ed treasured that watch; it was his talisman. To have it returned seemed so symbolic. A tangible sign. Surely it meant that he must be *dead*.

This time Mary couldn't hold back her tears. She covered her face with both hands.

'Mary—'

She could hear Tom's voice. His hand patted her arm tentatively and for a brief moment she thought how comforting it would be to cry on his shoulder. But, heavens, how inappropriate.

She sniffed loudly and dragged her arm over her face, trying to wipe her tears away on the sleeve of her shirt. 'I'm sorry,' she said. 'I'm not usually so fragile. It's such a strain, waiting to hear.'

'I'm sure it must be. Look, I'll just give the watch to you. I don't want to upset your son. And if he's not well he wouldn't want to have to meet a stranger.'

'That might be best.'

He reached into his shirt pocket and extracted a bulky envelope. 'There's no fancy packaging, I'm afraid.'

'Thank you,' she said softly, staring at the packet he held out to her, almost afraid to touch it. But as her fingers closed around it she said, 'I don't understand how Ed could give you this if he's disappeared.'

Tom grimaced. 'He wanted me to keep it safe for him till he got back from his last mission.'

'But he didn't come back?'

'No.' He avoided eye contact and bent down quickly.

For the first time she saw a box-shaped parcel covered in brown paper on the step at his feet. 'I knew the watch wouldn't mean a great deal to a little kid, so I bought him something else as well. A toy.'

'Tom, that's so thoughtful.'

He gave a dismissive shrug. 'It's no big deal. Ed and I were good mates so I wanted to do something for his son.'

Suddenly it felt wrong to keep this man standing on her doorstep. She had to forget about the past and the wild riot of feelings that tumbled through her. The past was behind them and the sane thing to do was to leave it there, locked away.

Her life and Tom's had taken different paths and they were different people now. These days Tom Pirelli was a good friend of her husband and he'd very thoughtfully brought Ed's son a gift.

That was how things were and how they must remain. Nothing more complicated than that.

She gestured to the box. 'This is very kind of you, Tom. You must come inside and give it to Ethan.'

'Are you sure it's OK?'

'Absolutely. I'll make some fresh coffee.'

'I must say I'd like to meet Ed's boy.'

Mary stepped back to allow Tom entry, and as he walked past her into the hall she drew a sharp breath. He was taller and more broad-shouldered than Ed and he seemed to fill the narrow hallway.

With the front door closed behind them she took Tom through to the kitchen, where the breakfast things were still on the table. Then she put the packet with Ed's watch on the counter and resisted the impulse to dash about madly trying to clear away cups and bowls and cereal packets. She didn't have to impress Tom; he hadn't come to check out her homemaking skills.

He stood in the middle of the room, holding the boxed gift in both hands.

'Ethan,' Mary called. 'We have a visitor.'

As the boy came running into the room her heart jolted painfully. Had Ed told Tom that he wasn't Ethan's biological father? She glanced from her son to Tom and saw the intense expression on Tom's face as he stared at the boy.

Oh, Tom, don't look like that.

For one horrible moment she thought the storm inside her might break through, but then she dragged in a deep breath and walked over to Ethan. The simple journey across her kitchen felt as dangerous as walking across thin ice, but once she reached the boy she drew him against her and brushed his fine blond hair with her trembling fingers.

'This is my little man,' she said, hoping her voice didn't sound as shaky as she felt. 'Ethan, honey, this is Tom. He's a friend of your daddy's.'

A brief frown creased Tom's brow when she said that, and she wondered if he expected her to add that he was also an old friend of hers. But they'd been so much more than friends and she *couldn't* say that.

'Hello, Ethan.' Tom smiled and held out his hand, while Ethan hesitated and leaned shyly against Mary's leg.

'Say hello to Tom,' she urged, giving him a gentle nudge.

'Hello, sir.' Ethan's big brown eyes seemed bigger than ever as his hand disappeared inside Tom's.

To Mary's surprise, Tom dropped to squat at Ethan's level as he offered him the box. 'Call me Tom,' he said.

'Hi, Tom.'

'Your Dad told me about you. I figured that you probably like knights in armour.'

The boy's eyes widened and he nodded solemnly.

'This is for you.'

To Mary's relief, her son remembered to say thank you without being prompted.

'Would you like a hand to open it?'

Ethan nodded and Tom set the box on the floor. For the next few moments the two males were silent and focused as they stripped the brown paper away and opened the box to reveal a toy castle, complete with towers, turrets and pennants. There was even a moat and a drawbridge.

'Wow!' exclaimed Ethan.

'The knights are inside,' Tom told him, and he swung a hinge that opened the castle.

'Wow!' Ethan breathed again as he reached in and drew out a model of a knight in shining plastic armour seated on a black horse. 'Oh, this is so neat.' He looked back to Mary, his eyes shining.

'Aren't you lucky?' she said.

'Is this from my dad?' Ethan asked. 'He said he'd bring me a present.'

Before Mary could set her son straight, Tom said without hesitation, 'Sure, mate, this is from your father.'

Ethan's eyes shone and Mary suppressed a choking sob.

'Now, these guys with bows and arrows go up in the keep,' Tom said, lifting out some models and setting them in place.

'And this one can be riding across the drawbridge,' Ethan chimed in excitedly.

Mary was so absorbed by the astonishing sight of

them together that at first she didn't notice the way her eyes were brimming with tears again. When a damp splotch rolled down her cheek she hurried away to clear the breakfast things and to make coffee.

After a while, Tom straightened again and left Ethan to play. He crossed the room to where Mary was taking a blue and white sugar bowl from an overhead cupboard.

His eyes drifted to her feet and his mouth quirked into a grim smile. Mary followed his gaze. Good grief! She was wearing one red shoe and one lime-green. Heavens, there must have been two pairs of slip-on shoes under the kitchen table and she'd taken no notice.

'So you still have trouble making decisions, Mary-Mary.'

'I jumped up to answer the door in a hurry,' she muttered as she crossed the room and extracted the odd shoes from under the table. She slipped off a lime-green shoe and swapped it for a red one. 'There, that's better,' she said, forcing a tiny laugh. 'At least I'm colour co-ordinated now.' She was wearing a red shirt and blue jeans.

She looked back towards Tom and their gazes linked. One corner of his mouth lifted into a tight, rueful smile. Was it her imagination, or could she see a shadowy sadness in his eyes as he looked at her for a long moment without speaking?

'Ethan looks like you,' he said at last. 'Same big brown eyes and soft blond hair.'

She nodded and gulped.

'Ed's mighty proud of him,' he added.

At the sound of his father's name Ethan's head snapped up. 'My dad's a Ranger,' he announced with pride.

'That's right, General.'

The boy's eyes grew huge and worried. 'Why did you call me General?'

'It just kind of slipped out. That's what your dad called you when he talked about you.'

Ethan's lower lip trembled.

'That was Ed's special nickname,' Mary explained. 'No one else called him General—only Ed.'

'I'm sorry. I didn't realise.' Tom walked back over to Ethan, bent down and touched him on the shoulder. 'Your dad and I were good mates.'

Don't talk in the past tense, Mary pleaded silently. *Ethan's very bright and he picks up on any subtleties.*

'Do you know when my dad's coming home?' Ethan asked.

'No,' Tom admitted with reluctance.

The light died in Ethan's eyes. He turned back to the knights and the castle and played with them quietly, keeping his head low, as if he needed to retreat. Sensing his mood, Tom backed away, but tension hovered in the air.

Mary fetched milk from the refrigerator and set it and the sugar bowl on the table. After a very short while Ethan asked her, 'Can I go back to watch TV?'

'I guess so,' she answered, nodding.

The boy hurried away and left the castle and its splendid knights on horseback lying abandoned in the middle of the kitchen floor.

Mary worried her lower lip with her teeth. 'He's not dealing very well with the bad news about his father,' she said.

'I dare say it will take a long time.'

She frowned. 'Why do you keep acting as if Ed's already dead? Surely, while there's a chance he's alive, we should hope?'

Tom kept his gaze fixed on the abandoned castle. 'I don't think there's much chance, Mary.'

'Why are you so sure?' she asked quietly. 'The Army has a great support network but I can't find out what happened. Were you there? Can you tell me?'

He swung his gaze back to hers and for the first time she saw how tired he looked. Smudges of shadow lay beneath his eyes and creases bracketed his mouth. 'We were involved in a hot extraction. You've heard about them, haven't you?'

'Where ropes are lowered from a helicopter?'

'That's it. Well, we'd finished a mission in the jungle and we were ready to be winched back up—'

'Where? Where was the mission?'

'South-East Asia.'

'But which country? Which jungle?'

'You should know better than to ask me that, Mary.'

She sighed. 'It was worth a try.'

'Anyway, the chopper was in position above us and we were below in the jungle and we had to get out fast. Really fast. There were guerrilla fighters all around us and it was pitch black. Even with night vision goggles we couldn't see a lot because of the dense timber, so we're not absolutely sure what happened. But somehow, when it was Ed's turn to ascend, the rope got tangled.'

'Oh, no,' Mary whispered.

'Sometimes trees, brush or ground debris can snag it. It hardly ever happens that the rope breaks, but it did this time.'

Mary flinched and tried to blot out the picture that formed in her head. 'So Ed fell,' she whispered.

'I'm afraid so.'

'But what happened then? Couldn't you find him?'

Tom heaved a loud, painful sigh.

'You did search for him, didn't you?'

'We tried, but we couldn't hang around for long. There was too much enemy fire. We had to consider the safety of the rest of the squad. And—' He looked as if he was about to say something else and changed his mind.

'So you just left him there?'

'Believe me, if I had my way I'd still be looking for him now, but that's not how the Army works. I had to follow orders. When I demanded permission to go back I had a run-in with the brass. A proper ding-dong confrontation.' He let out a hiss of air through gritted teeth. 'By the time I persuaded them that we should at least go back and recover his body there was no trace of him.'

Looking away from her, he stared through her kitchen window to a view across Arlington parkland. 'I think you should resign yourself to the fact that Ed won't be coming back, Mary. Everyone is convinced that he couldn't have survived that fall.'

She didn't answer, but she shook her head.

'I'm sorry,' Tom added, and his throat worked.

The smell of coffee filled the room and Mary distracted herself by collecting the coffee pot and their mugs and setting them on the cleared kitchen table. They took seats opposite each other and Mary felt painfully self-conscious. She wondered if Tom felt as awkward as she did to be sitting in such a domesticated setting— after all these years. It was so strange to be taking coffee with Tom Pirelli as if he were no more than a friend of Ed's.

Was he feeling as self-conscious as she was? Was he inwardly calm, or was he battling memories? She couldn't stop thinking about the past… Their past.

Good grief, here she was, worried about her husband,

and yet she was remembering it all. Dancing and laughing with Tom, kissing him, riding on the back of his motorbike, walking hand-in-hand with him in the moonlight along a beach of silver sand. Making love...

And then her father's insistence that Tom Pirelli couldn't possibly love her.

'Do you take cream or sugar?' she asked, forcing the memories aside.

'I'll have a little milk, no sugar, thanks.' He watched her fill his mug and then his face broke into a smile.

'What's amusing you?' she asked tightly.

'The way you call milk cream—like a proper Yank.'

She gave an offhand shrug. 'It happens when you spend eight years in a place. After a while you don't even notice the differences.'

'There are differences, though, aren't there?' he said, as if he were deliberately trying to steer their conversation into safe, pedestrian waters. 'I mean, on the surface Australians and Americans seem to speak the same language, but—'

'But here nappies are diapers and tomato sauce is ketchup.'

'Yeah—and footpaths are sidewalks and taps are faucets.'

'And scones are biscuits and biscuits are cookies.' Mary smiled too.

Tom watched her, then looked away and seemed to study her kitchen. It wasn't a remarkable kitchen but he took his time, as if he wanted to remember the yellow walls, white cupboards and sandstone-coloured bench tops, the decorative touches of blue and white pottery—Ethan's artwork stuck on the refrigerator door with magnets. On the wall, stars and stripes fashioned in cross-stitch framed the words 'God Bless America'.

'Ed's mother made that and gave it to us last Thanksgiving,' she said, feeling a need to explain.

She sat stiffly, twisting the coffee mug back and forth and not looking at him, aware that they would very quickly run out of safe topics to discuss. 'How is your Nonna?' she asked. 'I hope she's still alive.'

Fresh smile creases showed around his eyes and at the corners of his mouth. 'You bet she is. I think nonna's organised a special deal with God. No doubt she's promised him that when she gets to heaven she'll cook gnocchi gorgonzola on a regular basis, if he'll let her stay here till she's good and ready.'

'You've always loved your nonna's gnocchi gorgonzola, haven't you?'

'I'm surprised you remember.'

'Of course I remember.' *I remember everything about you, Tom.* 'Your nonna's very special.'

'Yeah.' Tom released a long sigh. 'It's too damn long since I've seen her.'

'Are you going back to Australia now?'

'Definitely. Soon as I can.'

The awkwardness returned and this time Tom must have decided he'd had enough. He jumped to his feet. 'Thanks for the coffee. I'd better get going.'

'Yes,' she said, jumping up just as quickly.

Was he happy to be leaving? Was that relief in his eyes? She remembered the way he used to smile whenever he saw her. The way his whole face would light up and his dark eyes would glow—and how she used to cling to him when it was time for them to part, begging for one more kiss—for him to hold her just a little longer.

And now they were both relieved to be parting.

He walked to the front door and she followed.

They said simple, unsatisfactory goodbyes without mentioning Ed again... Or their shared past.

Apart from the cold ache in her heart, there was nothing in the formal way they shook hands that suggested they had ever been lovers—nothing in the way she slipped her hand just a little too quickly from his that indicated that they had planned to marry.

Any second now, Tom would be turning away, walking out of her life. She knew this was best. His mission was accomplished. He'd brought the McBride family watch for Ethan and there was no more to do. Already she could sense his next move; he would execute a sharp about-turn and get the hell out of her home.

But he didn't move.

Instead, he stood on her front step and looked at her for ages. The muscles in his throat worked. 'Have you been happy, Mary?'

Oh, help! This was the one question in the world she didn't want to answer. And Tom was watching her so intently she feared he must see her sudden dismay. Had it shown in her eyes? Had it twisted her mouth downwards? She couldn't be disloyal to Ed now. He'd been a good husband. There was no one better. In a flash she recovered and sent Tom a bright smile.

'Of course I've been happy,' she said. 'You've met Ed, Tom. You know what a great guy he is. He's a very good man.'

'Sure,' Tom grunted. 'Ed's top shelf—he must have been a prize catch.'

He gave a curt nod and spun on his heel, at last eager to get away. Mary watched him and told herself she was glad he was leaving. It was best that they hadn't made any attempt to rake up the past. What was the point?

They couldn't go back. Parting without regret or recrimination was the adult way to behave.

But as Tom's foot touched the bottom step she felt the cruel weight of finality sink into her bones. Tom Pirelli was walking out of her life. A picture flashed before her of the last time she'd seen him, waiting on the corner, waiting to run away with her, to marry her.

And she heard herself calling suddenly, softly. 'What about you, Tom? Have you been happy?'

CHAPTER FOUR

THE fear came the very moment Mary asked the question.

Have you been happy? As soon as the words were out she felt a dreadful quaking terror deep inside. Why? Why couldn't she ask the question as easily as he had? And why was Tom staring at her with such a dark, accusing shadow in his eyes, as if he were angered by her question?

Was she imagining that sense of deep resentment that seemed to cling to him—as if it were a menacing presence that haunted him?

Was it guilt that made her so scared?

She had no cause to feel guilty. Eight years ago, on that night they'd tried to elope, Sonia had gone to Tom to explain why she couldn't meet him and Mary had waited for his answer. And waited... But there had been no word. And he'd never tried to contact her afterwards.

He hadn't suffered the agonies of disappointment that had made her so ill. He hadn't suffered in silent, lovesick misery the way she had. And he hadn't been left with a terrible, frightening secret. He knew nothing of the burden he had left her with, and he'd gone off to play heroes in the SAS without a backward glance in her direction.

Of course he'd been happy.

'I haven't been as happy as I should have been,' he said.

'Why?'

'How can *you* ask that, Mary?'

Her hand flew to her chest and her heart knocked. 'I don't understand. You can't be suggesting…'

Tom waited for her to finish. Mary couldn't breathe. This was a nightmare. He couldn't be telling her that he'd been unhappy all these years. Not because of her.

'You're not blaming me, are you?' she whispered.

'Why shouldn't I?'

'But, Tom, I didn't think you minded that I didn't go away with you. You just vanished without contacting me.'

His upper lip curled into a cold smile. 'Because that was what you wanted.'

'*What?*'

'Don't pretend you can't remember. You sent your cousin.'

'Yes, she went to tell you what happened. My father—'

'She came with the message that you didn't want to marry me.'

'No, she can't have.'

'You changed your mind, Mary-Mary.'

'No!'

'No?' Tom whispered.

'No way. You must have known. My father caught me and wouldn't let me out of the house. Of course I didn't change my mind. How could you think that?'

They stared at each other—the woman in the doorway, clutching the door handle to keep herself from falling; the soldier on the bottom step with a face so still it might have been carved from dark granite.

Mary's head swam and in the next heartbeat Tom was leaping up the steps, clasping her hands in his and drawing her back into the house.

'We have to talk,' he insisted, his voice choked, breathless.

'Not now, Tom,' Mary protested weakly. 'There's no point.'

The intensity in his eyes and the strength of his grip on her wrists frightened her. Talking to Tom about the past was dangerous.

Having him hold her like this was dangerous. She'd always been so susceptible to his touch.

No matter how hard she'd tried to forget, she remembered so much about Tom's touch. Heavens, she could even remember the first night she'd felt it—when she'd danced with him and the music had slowed and he'd drawn her close. She'd rested her head on his shoulder and she'd felt the whisper-soft brush of his lips on her temple just near her hairline.

How crazy that she'd remembered the electric thrill of that tiny caress through all these years. She mustn't think about it now.

'We have to talk. You owe me this, Mary,' he said quietly.

It was useless to pretend she didn't understand. The moment she'd asked Tom if he was happy she'd begun a conversation that had to be completed. She'd asked the first in a series of questions that had to be asked. And answered.

But what could they achieve besides heartache? There was no way they could go back. They couldn't undo the past eight years. And she was afraid of Tom, afraid of the power he'd always had over her.

Afraid he might somehow learn the truth about Ethan.

But, without another word, Tom led her back into the kitchen. They stepped around Ethan's castle and the scattered knights and he pushed her gently into a chair. Their empty coffee mugs were still sitting on the table where they'd left them. From the family room came the sounds of canned laughter and Mary thought guiltily that she mustn't let Ethan spend the whole morning watching television.

Tom sat opposite her with his elbows on the tabletop and his clenched fists pressed together. His dark eyes seemed to pierce her.

She took a deep breath. Best to get this over with. 'What did Sonia tell you that night my parents stopped me from going to you?'

'She said that you'd changed your mind, that at the last minute you'd hadn't been able to dredge up the courage to elope with me.'

'But that's not true. You didn't believe her, did you?'

Tom's gaze held hers for the longest time. She could see the way his eyes were searching her face, trying to gauge how honestly she was answering.

'No,' he said at last. 'I didn't believe her. I told her that I would be in touch with you, that we needed to talk it through and come up with a better plan.'

Mary pressed a hand against the pulse beating wildly at the base of her throat. 'Sonia didn't tell me that, Tom. She told me you were angry with me for chickening out—that you called me a tease.'

'The witch. I'd like to wring her scrawny neck.'

Mary sighed. 'It might cost you a packet. She's a lawyer these days and quite good at pressing charges.'

'That figures.'

'But, Sonia aside, what about your move to Perth? You never told me you'd applied for a transfer.'

'I didn't!' Tom shouted, then looked a little shame-faced and lowered his voice. 'Your father had me transferred. I had no choice.'

Mary stared at him as she came to grips with his news and the total injustice of what had happened. 'Dad convinced me that you were only pretending you wanted to marry me. He said it was some kind of payback because he refused your promotion. He said you'd already applied for a transfer to Perth.'

'Every word was a bloody lie. Your father had me transferred.'

'Oh, Tom. If only we'd been able to talk.'

'I tried to phone you.'

'My mobile phone mysteriously *disappeared* around that time.'

'Damn it, I tried everything, Mary. I hung around your house waiting to see you. I wrote letters. After I was transferred to Western Australia I even telephoned your house using a disguised voice, but I was told you wouldn't take my call. And when I tried to call again a few weeks later I was told that your father had been posted overseas and you'd moved to the States.'

'Dad managed to wangle a kind of exchange position at the Pentagon.' Mary hugged her arms over her chest. 'But you—you got on with your life, didn't you, Tom?'

'Yeah, I guess so.' He sent her a grimacing smile. 'I went out of my way to stop thinking about you. I disciplined my mind to cancel out thoughts of you. I just put you out of my mind.'

Was it easy, Tom? Mary's eyes and throat stung. Did she have the right to ask that question? On the surface it must look as if she'd had no trouble turning her back on Tom and creating a new life.

'I was so mad at my parents,' she said, needing to change the subject.

'But then you found Ed,' Tom said quietly. It wasn't an accusation, just a plain statement of fact.

'Yes.'

She'd been a single mother in a foreign country—surrounded by military families. She'd been so lonely and Ed's smile had been so warm. He'd been like a lighthouse—a friendly beacon for a shipwrecked sailor.

And, as it turned out, he'd needed her and Ethan as much as they had needed him.

'And what about you, Tom?'

'I told you I haven't been married.' He scratched his head and smiled sheepishly. 'I was engaged once, for twenty-four hours, but I was drunk when I proposed.'

Mary rolled her eyes. 'How come you've always had a reputation as a bad boy, and yet I've never seen that side of you?'

He cocked his head to one side and sent her a crooked, quizzical smile. 'Funny about that, isn't it?'

Mary looked away. Was he suggesting that she had the power to transform him?

'To be honest,' Tom said, 'I *was* a bit of a problem in your father's unit. There were things about the regular Army that drove me nuts—guard duty, drill parades, admin book work. But when I got to Perth, and they discovered I had good grades, was good at languages, but had a bit of a wild record, the SAS snapped me up. That suited me better—action all the time, interesting people—important projects like Afghanistan—Iraq.'

The telephone rang, startling Mary, and she jumped to answer it.

'Hi, honey,' came her mother-in-law's warm voice.

'Oh, Susan, hi.'

'I wasn't sure if I'd catch you before tennis.'

Oh, heavens. Mary glanced at the clock and remembered that she still hadn't rung to excuse herself from tennis this morning. 'I have Ethan at home with a cold,' she said.

She was aware of Tom standing, gathering up their coffee mugs. They made a slight rattling sound as he put them in the sink. Then came the sound of water running as he rinsed them.

'Do you have company?' Ed's mother asked.

'Actually, I have a visitor here who knows Ed,' Mary said as calmly as she could. 'He's from Ed's Special Squad.'

'Fancy that.' Susan McBride's voice quavered. 'Does he have any—any news?'

'He brought Ed's watch, Mom.'

'Oh, Mary. Oh, dear Lord. Does that mean...?'

'Tom doesn't know where Ed is. Ed gave him the watch just before their last mission.'

'Oh.'

During the stretch of silence that followed, Mary twisted the phone cord with nervous fingers.

'Will this man be here for long?' Susan asked. 'You must bring him down our way. How about coming to lunch on Sunday? Or perhaps tomorrow would be better if he's only here for a short stay. Frank and I would love to meet him.'

Mary hesitated. Clutching the phone receiver against her shoulder, she turned to Tom. 'Ed's mother has invited you to lunch on Sunday,' she said as casually as she could manage, trying to hide her reluctance to have him more deeply involved in her life. 'Or perhaps you'd prefer tomorrow.'

She prayed that he would refuse. How could she cope with the complication of Tom meeting Ed's parents? Every minute with Tom stirred the deep hidden feelings she'd worked so hard to bury, and she didn't know if she could hide her confusion with Ed's parents watching her.

Tom must be as anxious as she was to leave the past dead and buried behind them.

'Sure,' he surprised her by answering readily. 'Please tell Mrs McBride thank you. I'd like to meet Ed's parents. Tomorrow would be great.'

CHAPTER FIVE

As TOM strode down the hill away from Mary's apartment the undulating green parkland of Arlington National Cemetery stretched beyond the trees to his right. In the distance ahead of him he caught a glimpse of the slow, dignified curve of the Potomac River.

The sun was warm on his back and it was a relief to be walking. The way he felt right now he needed to walk all the way from Arlington right on to downtown Washington DC. Hell, finding Mary had him so wired with pent-up energy and angst he could walk clear across Virginia to Chesapeake Bay without stopping.

What a whacko world they lived in.

How could fate be so crazy that it led him to Mary Cameron again after eight long years, only to reveal that she was married to one of his best mates? And, damn it, she was a *mother* as well. Mother of his mate's son.

And the hell of it was, she was still able to cause him heartache. Mary had an extra aura of womanliness about her now, a Madonna-like softness and a mysterious, sensuous depth to her beauty that pierced him like a bayonet.

Ramming his hands into his trouser pockets, he flexed his shoulders and tried to release some of the building tension. Mary—*his* Mary. It shocked him to realise that he still thought of her as his. Damn fool that he was.

Eight years ago she'd been his for five months, but she'd discarded him. And he'd convinced himself that he was better off without her, that his feelings for her had only been puppy love.

Now he realised that his feelings had lain inside him like pieces of shrapnel, working their way slowly to the surface. Today they'd burst through, leaving raw, exposed wounds.

She loved Ed. Of course she would love the man. How could she not? Tom had befriended Ed McBride because he'd genuinely liked the guy. He'd come close to looking on Ed as a brother.

Now, he hadn't the heart to convince Mary that Ed wouldn't be coming home—couldn't bring himself to make her understand the realities of her husband's fall, or the horrors of what might have happened to him, even if he'd survived the drop. Why dash her hopes?

But already he was regretting that he'd accepted an invitation to lunch at her in-laws. It wasn't wise to get any more involved than he was already.

Mary McBride, aged twenty-eight, was not his Mary Cameron. She was a beautiful blonde with warm brown eyes who looked like his Mary, but she was a stranger— another man's wife and the mother of a little American boy. Tom had delivered the watch and now it was time to scarper home to his own family. They needed him more than the McBrides.

When he reached the bottom of the hill he crossed the busy main road and continued on walking. Walking and thinking. And, as he walked, the sun streamed on to the back of his neck and he found himself remembering another golden summer's morning when he'd been walking on Magnetic Island.

He'd been hiking back down the hilly track from the old Forts when he'd come across a young woman crouched on the ground. She had been marking a large arrow on the track out of broken gum twigs.

He must have looked especially puzzled when he'd

seen her because she'd rushed to explain what she was doing.

'There's a koala in the tree up there.'

Tom could still picture her kneeling on that track. Her pale golden hair plaited in a low braid, her body slender and lightly tanned, dressed in denim cut-offs and a red and white striped crop top, her face pretty and eager as she pointed up into the branches of the gum tree overhead.

She repeated her message very slowly, as if he were hard of hearing. 'A koala. Up there.' And she accompanied the words with effusive pantomime-style hand gestures. 'Look.'

Tom dropped his head back and looked high up into the fork of the gum tree and, sure enough, there was a fat ball of grey fur with raggedy ears—a koala asleep. 'You're dead right,' he said. 'Thanks for pointing it out.'

As soon as he spoke she jumped to her feet, blushing and brushing her hands on the back of her shorts as she hurried to explain. 'Sorry,' she gasped, looking and sounding flustered. 'I thought you were a backpacker from Europe or somewhere. There are so many here on the island and they all want to see koalas, so they appreciate it if we mark any sightings for them.'

'I'm sure they do,' Tom assured her, smiling. About to walk on, he paused and asked, 'So you're in the tourism business?'

'Oh, no. My parents have a weekender here on the island, so I often come over from Townsville for a getaway.' She pointed to the arrangement of sticks. 'These koala markers are a kind of island tradition.'

Tom grinned and nodded. Took a deep breath. Knew he should continue walking, but hunted for another question to put to her instead. 'So this arrow is your good deed for the day?'

She smiled and shrugged. 'Perhaps.'

'Are you on your way up or down the track?'

He was almost certain that she hadn't been to the top yet, and she hesitated for just a fraction and then said, 'I'm heading back down.'

He nodded and grinned again. And she smiled back at him. Her eyes were a lovely warm brown—a rich, welcoming colour, with warm honey highlights and deep soul shadows—eyes he suddenly wanted to get lost in.

'Want company?' he asked.

She smiled shyly. 'Sure.'

By the time they got to the bottom of the walking track Tom knew that her name was Mary Cameron and that she was in her third year of studying Business and Marketing. It was a relief to hear that. It meant she had to be at least twenty.

He told her that his grandparents were migrants from Italy.

'So I wasn't too far off track when I thought you were a backpacker,' she said, laughing.

'Only by a generation or two.'

They laughed together—and their eyes met—and Tom realised with a shock that they were making a very special kind of connection. Not mere flirting. It felt beyond that.

He told her that he was in the Army, but she didn't mention that her father was also in the forces. When they reached the end of the walking track he asked her out on a date—and that was when she looked at his motorbike and suddenly became nervous and shy.

And she declined his invitation.

Mary was pleased that Ethan agreed to a nap after lunch, until she realised that his silence left her alone with her thoughts. It had been hard enough holding unwanted images at bay all morning while she'd conscientiously entertained Ethan. They'd sprawled on the carpet in the family room and had played with the castle that Tom brought and they'd read all Ethan's favourite books and played several games of dominoes.

But every time Ethan had looked up at her with his piercing dark brown eyes she'd seen Tom.

Until now, everyone had always commented that Ethan looked like her—and superficially they did look alike. The fact that they both had blonde hair and brown eyes helped to cement the idea. But now that Mary had seen Tom again she was worried. The expression in Ethan's eyes and the way he held his mouth were so very much like Tom that she feared any outsider would notice the likeness instantly.

When her son frowned in concentration she saw Tom. And when he looked wide-eyed and questioning, or when he smiled at her, she saw Tom...

Had Tom noticed? Would others notice?

And would they also notice how shaken she was by Tom's presence? Oh, Lord. She felt twenty again.

Tom Pirelli had walked into her kitchen and the image she'd so carefully created over the past five and a half years—Mary McBride, contented wife and mother—had begun to fracture from the inside out.

And she'd thought she'd done such a good job of reclaiming her life.

It hadn't been easy. Soon after they'd arrived in America there'd been a horrendous battle with her father when she'd refused to have an abortion.

'I don't want my grandson tainted by Tom Pirelli's genes,' her father had told her.

She'd grown up that day. Her disgust at his outburst had forced her to realise that she must take responsibility for her own life. And for her baby's life. From then on she'd worked hard to establish her independence and to assert herself.

Knowing that her father would never change, she'd moved into her own accommodation after Ethan was born and she'd struggled to make ends meet by establishing her marketing business, working from home.

Of course, her father had fought her move with emotional blackmail, accusing her of deserting them—of ruining her mother's happiness.

No wonder she'd welcomed Ed into her life.

Her stomach churned as she closed Ethan's bedroom door and wandered back through the house. Ahead of her stretched a long summer afternoon and feverish, torturous memories.

She went down to the kitchen and made herself a cup of coffee, then carried it back up to her study. There, she switched on her computer and opened her e-mail messages, determined to concentrate on the communications from her clients.

But, within minutes, the words on the screen faded. Memories stormed her mind like battering rams breaking down a castle door. She sat with her elbows resting on the desktop and her hands pressed against her eyes. She didn't want to think about Tom.

Think about Ed.

She'd known from the start that she and Ed would never have the same kind of sensuous, passionate relationship she'd had with Tom. In a way, theirs had been a marriage of convenience, a compromise for both of them. She'd needed Ed's warmth, his compassion and support. And Ed had needed a ready-made family.

Before he'd proposed to her Ed had told her that he was sterile and, although she'd been sorry, she'd also been relieved, because it meant she had something to offer him. Her gift of Ethan would make up for any lack of fire in their relationship.

Ed had become a wonderful father figure—so proud of Ethan and a great role model for the boy. And she'd done everything in her power to become a good wife.

There had been genuine love between them.

Not setting-the-world-alight passion, but warm, deep affection.

The problem was, thinking about this didn't help her at all, because these thoughts brought her back to Tom again. She kept picturing the last time she'd seen him, when she was standing at her bedroom window, looking down at him as he waited for her on the footpath.

Concentrate on your work.

She stared hard at the computer screen. There were several messages she needed to send. She began to type, telling one client, a paint company, that she'd sent the designs for their brochures to the printer and assuring another that she'd placed the dance company's advertisement in the *Washington Post*. And she informed someone else she could meet this deadline…

But it was no good.

She gave up trying to fight the pictures in her head, letting her mind trail right back to the beginning… To the day she'd met Tom on a walking track.

She'd been overcome by shyness and she'd hurried away from him that day. However, fate had had other plans…

Quite unexpectedly they'd met again, at a nightclub, on her cousin Sonia's eighteenth birthday.

Sonia had persuaded Mary and a group of friends to accompany her to the nightclub to celebrate being able to drink alcohol legally. The club had been typically noisy and crowded and dark and, as Mary had sipped her margarita she'd caught sight of Tom Pirelli through the flickering flashes of the strobe lighting.

She had been startled by the sudden jolt she'd felt when she'd seen him sitting at the bar with a group of his mates. It had been so weird. She had caught one glance of Tom Pirelli across the dimly lit, crowded and smoky room and felt as if she were being launched into outer space.

When he had looked her way and recognised her he had sent her a slow, sexy smile and quicksilver shivers had turned her arms to goosebumps.

'Who's that?' Sonia asked.

'Just some guy in the Army.'

'Oh, an Army Jerk,' her cousin replied with a dismissive sniff. 'A-Js are the dregs.'

Mary marvelled that Sonia could make such a comment when her uncle, Mary's Army officer father, was providing her with free board and lodging. But she knew that a lot of girls shared Sonia's attitude. And it was true that some of the young soldiers were pretty wild.

Which was why admiring Tom from a safe distance was one thing, but when she saw that he was coming towards her—across the dark, crowded room—zigzagging through the dancing couples—her heart began to pound crazily.

He was so darkly handsome and Italian and dangerous looking. Just as he reached her the band started a noisy number and, although he raised his voice, Mary couldn't hear him.

Tom had to lean close to speak directly into her ear and she could smell his skin—a nice, clean, lightly spiced smell that might have been aftershave, she wasn't quite sure. All she knew was she liked it.

'You look as if you're afraid of me,' Tom said loudly.

'Do I?' she yelled back, knowing it was true.

'You shouldn't be,' he shouted. 'I have very good family credentials.' He grinned. 'You should ask my nonna some time. She'll tell you I'm a Very Nice-a Boy.'

Mary laughed. And she suspected she couldn't resist Tom a second time. She was already halfway in love with the way he looked, and now he'd made her relax and laugh.

So they danced.

The loud noise from the band made conversation difficult, so they danced, exchanging smiles, with very little touching.

When the other girls came to tell her they'd grown tired of this nightclub and wanted to move on to another, Tom offered to take Mary home. But she saw the pouting droop of Sonia's mouth and she felt guilty. It was her cousin's birthday and she was spending all night with Tom. So she told him she couldn't abandon her friends and headed with them for the door.

She tried very hard to put Tom out of her mind in the weeks that followed. What was the point of getting all worked up about a guy she'd had a couple of dances with?

And then, one Sunday morning, she went into the Cotters' Markets in Flinders Mall to look for a gift for a friend who was leaving town. Strolling past the stalls, she was admiring the arts and crafts and the barrows of tropical fruit and flowers from local farms, when she heard a male voice calling out her name.

And she turned and saw Tom and an elderly woman standing behind one of the stalls.

Zap! The minute she saw him, she reacted as if she'd been hot wired. But this time she felt confident enough to wave and cross over to speak to them.

'Doing some shopping?' Tom asked when she reached them.

'Mostly browsing. What are you doing here?'

'I'm giving my nonna a hand.' He half turned to the tiny woman beside him. 'Nonna, this is Mary. Mary, I'd like you to meet Gina Pirelli, the fierce matriarch of the Pirelli dynasty.'

Tom's little nonna was very brown and wrinkled, with soft brown hair streaked with grey and jet-black eyes exactly like her grandson's. But, as far as Mary could see, there was nothing fierce about her. Her dark eyes twinkled with warmth and her smile was wide.

'Hello, Mary.' She spoke with a strong Italian accent.

'Lovely to meet you, Mrs Pirelli.' Mary glanced at the products they were selling and saw grey packets labelled *Pirelli Tea* in black. From what she'd learned in her Business and Marketing degree, she was quite certain that the tea could have been packaged more attractively, but prudently refrained from offering an opinion. 'Does your family grow tea?' she asked them.

'Yes,' Tom's nonna answered, holding out a packet to her. 'You should buy. It is very good for your health. It's natural organic tea grown on our plantation on the Atherton Tableland.'

'I'd love some,' Mary said, digging into the bottom of her woven shoulderbag for her purse.

When the transaction was complete Tom kept his smiling gaze on Mary as he gave his grandmother a one-armed hug. 'Nonna, can you persuade this young lady that she should go out with me?'

Zap, zap, zap! Mary thought she might have a heart attack.

The old woman's dark eyes widened and for a disquieting moment she studied Mary, her twinkling black eyes surveying her from head to toe. 'You don't want to go out with my Toto?'

'Well— I—' Mary stammered and blushed.

'She's frightened of me,' Tom said.

'Cautious rather than frightened,' Mary corrected.

Nonna waggled a finger in her face. 'You got to trust my grandson. Look how good he is. He helps me with this stall. He's a Very Nice-a Boy.'

'Are you absolutely certain of that?' Mary asked her, suppressing a fierce desire to grin, because Tom was grinning and winking at her from behind his grandmother's back.

Gina Pirelli looked as if she were choking on air. 'Of course he's a nice-a boy. He's my grandson. I know these things.'

'That's very reassuring,' Mary said, smiling now. In fact, they all had a jolly good chuckle, and Gina Pirelli pinched Tom's cheek and then Mary's cheek for good measure.

'I like this one, Toto,' Gina said.

And Mary bought two more packets of Pirelli tea and fell the rest of the way in love with Tom Pirelli right there in the middle of the market.

And when he walked with her to the end of the row of market stalls and asked her out, she said yes.

That evening they went dancing again, and when the music slowed and Tom drew her close she was ready and eager and *hungry* for the feel of his arms around her. They moved slowly, breathlessly, cheek to cheek, thigh to thigh. The proximity of Tom's toned, muscular body made her insides melt. His soft lips brushed her forehead, close to her hairline. He kissed the back of her neck.

She tingled from head to toe as they drifted towards a shadowy corner and he said softly, 'Don't worry,

Mary, I'm going to be very well-behaved. It's just that my lips have a thing for your lips.'

'They do?' she asked in a languorous, almost dreamy voice. Truth was, she no longer minded if he wasn't all that well-behaved.

Then he kissed her. And he took a delicious, bone-melting, breath-stealing long time…

'Mummy.'

'Oh!'

Ethan's voice jerked Mary out of her daydream so suddenly she almost fell off her swivel chair. He was standing in the study doorway. 'Ethan, what do you want?'

'I'm not tired any more. Can I get up?'

She glanced at her watch. Almost an hour had passed since she'd put him to bed. The coffee cup beside her was still half full, but it had grown stone cold. 'How are you feeling?' she asked him.

'I think I'm better.'

'No more nonsense,' Mary chided later that night as she tucked Ethan into bed for the third time. 'You're to stay here this time.'

'I'm not sleepy,' he complained, even though his eyelids drooped heavily.

'Close your eyes and think of something you'd really like to see,' she said. 'Think about your favourite things.'

Thick black lashes curled against soft pink cheeks as the boy's eyelids drifted closed.

'What do you see?'

'I see my dad's face,' he said.

'Oh, sweetheart, that's good. What else? What else do you see?'

'Grandpa's red rooster.'

'Yes… And anything else? Keep looking for nice things.'

'And I can see the castle. The one Dad sent me.'

'Tom brought it for you, darling.'

Ethan's eyes flashed open. 'But I know it's really from Dad, Mummy. Isn't it cool? None of my friends have a castle like that, with knights and swords and horses and a proper drawbridge.'

'It's wonderful, darling,' Mary whispered. 'Now, close your eyes again and dream about your lovely castle and I'll stay here beside you for a little while.'

The boy hugged her and rolled sleepily on to his side, and she sat in the soft lamplight. Thinking about Tom and Ed and the castle.

She knew Ed would never have bought a gift like the castle. Ed was a dear man, but he'd never been a romantic. If he'd sent his son a gift it would have been something like a baseball mitt, a fishing line, or a football. Not a fairytale castle.

It had been rather generous of Tom to let Ethan think that the gift came from his father.

It had come from his father. His biological father.

But neither of them knew that.

'Oh, what a sad mess this is,' she whispered almost soundlessly. What was she going to do?

CHAPTER SIX

VISITING Ed's parents was a big mistake. From the moment Tom got out of the car in front of the McBrides' place he could feel his frustration brewing. Somehow his simple plan to return a watch to the son of a mate lost in action was getting out of hand.

Meeting Mary again had thrown him completely off course. Over the years he'd managed to bury his feelings for her, but one look at her yesterday and his youthful passion had been exposed and brought to the surface—intact—and as powerful as ever.

He'd be fooling himself if he didn't admit that he'd accepted this invitation because of a burning need to see more of her. But the reality was he was getting too close to a family tragedy.

Mary must have sensed the lowering of his mood. 'Don't worry, Tom. Ed's parents are very nice, easy-going folk,' she said, as they waited for Ethan to unhook his seat belt and scramble out of the back seat. 'They're coping well and they're not into heavy sentimental scenes.'

He didn't answer as he took a long, hard look at the McBrides' home.

It was just as he'd pictured the place where Ed had grown up—a neat, traditional, two-storey house with shining white clapboard walls, grey shutters, shingle roof and cute front porch. From the watermelon-pink blaze of the crepe myrtle tree near the front steps to the proud red, white and blue flag flapping bravely in the Virginian sunshine, it was picture-perfect.

But entering this house, seeing Mary with Ed's folks, seeing how much a part of their family she was, would be a different matter. And suddenly the idea of being cosy with Mary's in-laws felt wrong.

Why the heck had he accepted the invitation so readily?

Tom thought of his own parents' farm on a misty green hill slope on the Atherton Tableland in North Queensland. Mary would have fitted in there. No problem.

He swallowed the stone in his throat. He felt so alien here. He *was* alien. He was an outsider in this woman's life, and the knowledge ripped at his heart.

As soon as Susan McBride walked into the front room she knew why Mary had sounded as if she had lightning bugs jumping inside when she'd spoken on the phone yesterday. The truth hit her with a certainty that almost sent the pitcher of lemonade she carried crashing to the floor.

The visiting Australian had Ethan's eyes.

Or, more correctly, Ethan had eyes exactly like this man's. There was no doubt; the likeness was as familiar and striking as the stars and stripes flag.

Susan's hand shook and the ice cubes rattled violently in the glass pitcher as she set it down. She had always known that Ethan's father was Australian, but she'd never expected to meet him. *Had Frank noticed the likeness?*

It didn't seem so, she decided, as her husband shepherded Mary, Ethan and Tom Pirelli into the front room, happily chatting about the heat as he tousled Ethan's hair.

'You all find yourselves a seat now,' he said, offering their guest the comfortable recliner by the window, right by the electric candle she'd set on the windowsill. The candle that shone each evening. For Ed.

Susan's hand felt cold as she offered it in greeting. 'Welcome, Captain Pirelli.'

'Thank you, Mrs McBride, but please call me Tom.'

'If you'll call me Susan.'

He smiled at her and his teeth flashed white in his tanned face. His handshake was firm and friendly, as was his smile. But those eyes! Not the warm honey-brown of Mary's, but so dark they were almost black—piercing black. Just like Ethan's.

What did this mean? Glancing towards Mary, Susan saw that she was looking pale and strained. And Susan felt suddenly cold and fearful, as if the summer's day had receded and wintry rain had begun to drizzle through her.

'Grandma!'

Two small arms wrapped around her waist and a sturdy warm body pressed against her. 'Hey, darling,' she cried, reaching down to hug her grandson close. 'How is my big boy today?'

Ethan hugged her tight and then tighter and she buried her face in his soft golden hair. He smelled of shampoo and summer. How she loved this little boy. At times Susan wondered if she'd loved her own children so fiercely. When they were little she'd been forced to juggle her motherly love with the necessary discipline and duty of raising a child, but as a grandmother she'd given herself total freedom to love Ethan without limits.

As Susan released the boy and straightened she was

aware of Tom Pirelli watching her closely. She smiled down at Ethan. 'How would you like to collect the hens' eggs for me?'

'You bet!'

'Be careful now,' she called after him as he dashed outside. Then she turned just a shade too briskly back to the adults. 'Let me pour everyone some lemonade. Or would you prefer iced tea, Mary?'

'Lemonade will be just fine, thank you.'

'Tom, what will you have?'

'Lemonade, please.'

'I suppose you'd rather have beer?'

'No, lemonade sounds great.'

'Are you sure?'

Frank looked aggrieved. 'Susan, stop fussing and pour the man a drink.'

After the drinks were poured and the weather discussed, Susan made an excuse to hurry back to the kitchen to give finishing touches to their salad.

'Can I help?' Mary called after her.

'That would be lovely, honey.'

Mary followed her mother-in-law and her heart thudded. She'd made good friends with Susan and could read her moods well. She'd noted the strange look on her face when she'd seen Tom. And, as Ed's mother was never one to beat about the bush, chances were her thoughts would come out into the open before lunch was over. Best to deal with it now, in the privacy of the kitchen. Away from Ethan. And Tom.

'I've made chowder and lump meat crab cakes,' Susan said. 'I just have to reheat them and finish the salad.'

'Wonderful. Now what can I do?'

'Can you slice these tomatoes?'

'Of course.'

Susan handed Mary a chopping board and a sharp knife, but the tension in her eyes caused Mary's heart to thump.

'Does he know?' Susan hissed.

Struggling to hide her shocked dismay, Mary stammered, 'H-he? Who are you t-talking about?' After all, there were three males out there.

'You know I'm talking about Tom Pirelli. Those eyes, Mary. They're so much like Ethan's.'

'Yes, they are, aren't they?' Mary took a deep breath and arranged the board and the knife and the tomatoes on the bench in front of her. 'Isn't it weird?' She picked up the knife. 'Do you want wedges or slices?'

'Wedges will be fine,' Susan muttered impatiently. 'So tell me there's no connection between this Australian and Ethan. Is the likeness a fluke, a coincidence?'

Mary stopped cutting.

Her head whirled. Panic threatened, but she suspected that if she lied about this she would feel ten times worse. She needed to tell Susan the truth. 'There's a connection.' She spoke slowly, so there could be no mistake. 'The only coincidence is that Tom's turned up in my life again now.'

Her mother-in-law let out a long sigh as she leaned back against the cupboards. Folding her arms across her chest, she studied Mary. 'So I'm asking you again, does he know?'

'No,' Mary said as she resumed slicing a tomato into even wedges.

'Are you sure? Has the man had his eyesight tested? You mean he hasn't noticed that the boy's the spitting image of himself?'

'He thinks Ethan looks like me.'

Susan's shoulders relaxed and she nodded slowly. 'I

guess that's possible. The blond hair helps. We always thought Ethan looked like you.' She turned to the sink and began to rinse lettuce leaves. 'I presume you haven't said anything to Ethan?'

'Good heavens, no.'

'How has he reacted to Tom?'

Mary sighed. 'Actually…not very well. He doesn't understand why Tom can come home and Ed can't. He's frightened of what it means and he resents Tom.'

After several minutes of silence Susan said, 'If Tom hasn't guessed anything, you don't need to tell him, do you?'

The knife slipped in Mary's hand. 'Ouch!'

'What happened?'

'It's OK,' Mary said, examining her thumb. 'I didn't actually cut myself. It was just a close call.' She picked up the knife again. 'Don't you think Tom deserves to know about his son?'

'No, I don't. Think about it, Mary. You didn't tell him way back when you were pregnant, so why should you now?'

We were forced apart. I didn't know until it was too late. I swallowed the lies my father fed me.

It was too complicated to try to explain all that in a hurry.

'Honey,' said Susan, 'you obviously didn't want this Tom as the father of your child when you had the chance. And now you owe much more to poor Ed. Saints preserve us, think what bringing all this out into the open would do to him. Ed loves your boy. Ethan's *his* son now. Ed's been a fantastic father—his only father—the best.'

'I think you're probably right,' Mary said softly. 'I have to think of Ethan.' But privately Mary just didn't know what was right or wrong in the whole situation any more. She carried the wedges of tomatoes to the salad bowl. 'But, Susan, I'm afraid… Tom doesn't hold out much hope for Ed.'

Susan flinched, then squared her shoulders and eyed Mary fiercely. 'I'm not listening to that kind of talk. I have no intention of giving up hope. Every house in this street has a candle burning in their front window for Ed. He's coming home, Mary. You have to believe that.'

'Yes, of course.' She looked around for another task. 'What kind of dressing are you going to put on that?'

'There's a nice Italian dressing on the top shelf of the refrigerator. Could you get it, dear?'

'Sure.' Mary collected the bottle and handed it to Susan. 'What if Tom asks me about Ethan's age? He'll be sure to guess then.'

'Cross that bridge when you come to it. Young bachelors can be very vague about the ages of children. It's not something that looms large on their need-to-know list.'

The kitchen door swung noisily open and Ethan rushed in and held a small metal bucket out to Susan. 'I found four eggs, Grandma, and I remembered to shut the hens' door.'

The two women exchanged a significant look and Mary noticed the happiness shining in Ethan's eyes and realised that he showed no sign of having a cold today.

In the sitting room, Ed's father pressed Tom for details about Ed's situation, and Tom, as briefly as he could, told him what he'd told Mary—that Ed couldn't have survived the fall.

Frank McBride didn't fight the news the way Mary had. He accepted it quietly and for several minutes sat without speaking, staring at the woven rug on the floor in front of him. 'Ed told me it would be a robust engagement,' he said, still staring sadly at a spot beyond his feet. 'I knew that was a euphemism for a very tough two-way battle—probably the toughest warfare he'd encountered so far.'

'Your son was a brilliant and brave soldier,' Tom said, 'and I truly valued his friendship.'

The men sipped their cool drinks in solemn silence and Tom's gaze drifted to the photos of the McBride family that vied for pride of place on the sideboard, alongside a summery arrangement of roses and day lilies. There were several shots of Ethan at different stages between toddlerhood and the present day, as well as wedding photos of a young couple Tom didn't recognise and a close-up head and shoulders shot of Mary and Ed.

He felt a pang of dismay. Mary had been a breathtakingly beautiful bride. The misty veil only served to make her look lovelier than ever. His hungry eyes took in every detail—the golden curls framing her face, the dainty white flowers pinned in her hair, the glow in her dark eyes and the radiance of her smile.

And Ed looked incredibly damned happy. Hell, the man was beaming so proudly Tom felt his eyes sting. He gripped the lemonade glass so tightly his fingers almost crushed it.

'That was a happy day,' Frank said, noting the direction of Tom's gaze. 'Mary's a first-rate daughter-in-law.'

Tom nodded and swallowed, trying to ease the sharp pain in his throat.

'She's smart as paint,' Frank went on. 'Her skills are in high demand in her marketing business, but she's been careful to balance her work with caring for Ethan.

And, although Ed's away so much, she always makes time to visit us.'

'That's great,' Tom said. Then, needing to divert his host's attention, he asked, 'Who's the other couple?'

'That's our daughter, Paula, and her husband, Bill. They live in San Francisco now, so we don't see as much of them as we'd like to—although I'm sure that's going to have to change very soon.' Frank smiled. 'Paula's expecting. Her littl'n is due next month and Susan's beside herself. There's no way she'll sit here in Virginia when there's a grandbaby to fuss over on the west coast. She's been longing for another grandchild. You know— one of our own—'

There was a coughing sound in the doorway. Susan was standing there. 'Lunch is ready,' she announced rather loudly, and both men jumped to their feet.

Ethan put on a turn when it was time to go home, and Mary felt so tense and strung-out after sharing a meal with Tom and Ed's parents that she handled it badly.

'I don't want to go home with you and Tom,' the child told her, sending Tom a baleful glare. 'I want to sleep over at Grandma's. Please, Mummy, please.'

Mary winced. She hated it when Ethan used that pitiful, whining tone. It was a new tactic he'd developed since the bad news had come through about Ed, and she still wasn't sure if she should pity her son or be cross with him for manipulating her.

And today, with Tom watching her and with the knowledge that if she left Ethan behind she would be alone with Tom, she felt even more unsure. On most occasions like this she would have already discussed the possibility of a sleepover with Susan, but today her mother-in-law had remained silent on that subject, and now she made no comment as she watched from the sidelines with wary eyes.

It was Frank who spoke up. 'Let the boy stay, Mary. We don't see enough of him since he's started school, and you know he's always welcome here. Susan has his bed made up and his pyjammies ready, and I can easily run him back home to you tomorrow afternoon.'

'Yes, Grandpa, yes!' cried Ethan excitedly.

'I don't know...' Mary hedged. She looked towards Tom and the ebony fire in his eyes made her feel as if she'd stepped on to a spinning merry-go-round.

But it seemed that Frank and Ethan had already made the decision for her. While Susan watched, with arms folded across her chest and mouth firmly buttoned, Ethan danced a jig around his grandfather, holding his hands and cheering.

With that settled, there was little to do but to give Ethan instructions to be on his best behaviour, to thank Susan for lunch and to say goodbye. It all happened very quickly and in no time at all Mary was in the car, heading back up the highway.

Alone with Tom.

Very tense and alone with Tom.

She gripped the steering wheel while he lounged back in the passenger seat and idly watched forests of oak, maple and pine flash past. She couldn't help wondering if he was remembering their journeys of old, the times she'd ridden on the back of his motorcycle with her hands slipped beneath his leather jacket as she clung to him for dear life.

If only she wasn't so painfully aware of his physical presence now. An older, sexier Tom Pirelli. Here. Sitting beside her. Alone with her. Touching close.

'Ethan's a cute kid.'

His comment seemed to come out of nowhere, wrenching her back from fantasy to the real world.

'I'm worried that I'm spoiling him,' she said.

'I'm no expert, but he seems normal to me. You should see my brother's kids. They can get pretty wild at times.'

'I'd almost forgotten you had a brother. How is he?'

Tom drew a deep breath and the fingers of his right hand tapped his knee as he expelled it. 'Stefano lost a leg in a tractor accident a couple of years ago.'

Mary shot him a look of horror. 'That's terrible.'

'Yeah.'

'I'm so sorry to hear that. Is he OK?'

'It was touch and go for a while, but he's made a good recovery.' To Mary's surprise, Tom chuckled. 'Actually, he's made a great recovery. He has a prosthesis and is mobile again, and he dines out on stories about how he lost the leg.'

She smiled. 'I suppose he tells people a crocodile ate it?'

'You've got it,' Tom said, returning her smile. 'Most times he claims that he lost it fighting a crocodile in the Kimberley, or sometimes it happened when his fishing boat capsized and he had to do battle with a Great White shark.'

'But a tractor accident must have been just as frightening.'

'Yes, he was ploughing a steep slope and the tractor rolled, but he managed to tie a tourniquet around his leg. He virtually saved his own life.'

'Wow! So the Pirelli family have two heroes.'

Their gazes caught and Mary felt the full force of the magnetic attraction that had brought them to the brink of marriage. It zinged between them, stronger than ever. Oh, help! Tom mustn't look at her like that.

The space inside the car seemed to contract and she felt fire running through her veins, heating her skin, filling her head with steam.

Wrenching her eyes to the front again, she forced herself to focus on the road ahead and the world beyond the car. They were passing close by water now. She caught a swift impression of hire boats and a waterside café with tables and chairs set beneath green and white umbrellas.

She took a deep breath and spoke as calmly as she could. 'I guess your family have had to manage the farm without your brother?'

'They've been trying to manage, but it's been tough. Dad wants to retire, and he's been at me to leave the Army and come home.'

'But that's not what you want?'

Tom took his time answering. 'As a matter of fact…it's exactly what I want.'

Her hands tightened on the steering wheel. 'You mean you're leaving the SAS?'

'Yep. The idea of leading a more sedate life is beginning to have big appeal. I like the idea of getting up in the morning and doing much the same things as I did yesterday and as I'm going to do tomorrow. I'm going home to settle down and grow tea on the green, green hills of Millaa Millaa.'

'Goodness, Tom. I don't think of you as a domesticated animal.'

She sensed him turn her way. 'How do you think of me, Mary?'

The weight of irony in his voice made her flustered.

'I mean, it's hard to picture you running a tea planta-tion.'

'I can assure you it's a damn sight prettier than what I've been doing for the past decade.'

'I guess so,' she admitted, but she felt distinctly un-settled to think of Tom going home to Australia, living a peaceful life in the bosom of his family. No doubt he would want to start a family of his own.

Without warning, she was remembering the time they'd taken the crazy risk that had brought Ethan into the world. On impulse she'd taken Tom to the cottage on the island and a fierce storm had hit. It had sprung out of nowhere, catching everyone by surprise. Ferry trips back to the mainland had been cancelled and they'd had to stay overnight.

They had been completely swept away by the sweet, wild intimacy of making love while the storm hurled rain and palm fronds against the cottage windows.

Stop it! Don't think about it.

Needing a distraction, she reached over to switch on the radio, but her hand froze in mid-air when Tom said, 'Excuse me for prying, but was it from choice that you and Ed only had one child?'

Oh, help. Not now, not this topic. Please, Tom...

She dampened her dry lips with her tongue. Why had she made that promise to Susan? Keeping the truth about Ethan from Tom felt so bad. Was Susan right? Would she be betraying Ed if she told Tom? If Ed was still alive...

'Mary?'

'We—we would have liked a playmate for Ethan.'

'What went wrong?'

'It's just one of those things. Ed and I haven't been able to have a baby.'

'But you have Ethan.'

'Y-yes.' Fear and confusion made her rush to explain. 'But we haven't been able to have *another* baby. I've worried myself sick. You hear so much about mothers giving an only child too much attention. And I felt so intense about Ethan. I guess another baby would have helped to—to dilute my maternal feelings, but—but it didn't turn out that way.'

She risked a fleeting sideways glance in Tom's direction and saw that he was staring straight ahead, his face hard and expressionless. *What was he thinking?* Her hands were so sweaty they threatened to slip off the steering wheel and she hoped he didn't notice as she wiped them one at a time on her skirt.

Tom deserved to know about his son. Should she tell him? It was seemed so unfair to hold back.

The traffic was getting heavier now, as they approached the outskirts of DC, and she kept her eyes carefully on the road. As the car rushed on and Tom sat, wrapped in his own thoughts, Mary wrestled with her conscience. The more she thought about it, the more sure she was that Tom should know.

Yes, she would tell him. Now.

She opened her mouth, ready to confess. Then shut it again as another thought struck. Tom had just finished telling her that he wanted to go home to Australia to start a new life. If she told him about Ethan now, after all these years, would he mistrust her motives? Would he think she was trying to tie him to her?

Perhaps it was best to say nothing after all. That way she wouldn't betray Ed. And Tom wouldn't feel trapped.

It might be wiser to play it safe for now, but she promised herself that some time in the future, if news came through that Ed had died, horrible as that thought was, she would owe it to Ethan and to Tom to reveal the truth.

With that decision made she felt a little better, but just the same the secret hovered over her like a black, guilty ghost.

The afternoon sun was losing its impact by the time they entered Washington DC. Shadows were lengthening across the city's parks and she was both relieved and dismayed that she and Tom were nearing the end of their journey.

Perhaps Tom was thinking about that too, because suddenly he asked, 'Have you seen the Lincoln Memorial?'

'Yes, of course. Several times. Ed and I nearly always take our out-of-state visitors to see it.'

'I was wondering if you could take me there? Is it far out of your way?'

'No. I—I guess we could go there.'

'I have an urge to stand on those steps and look up at the big guy and read his famous words. You know—about "a new nation conceived in liberty" and all that.'

'It is very moving.'

'And I might not be back this way in a long time.'

Mary blinked as her vision blurred. 'I guess you won't.'

She parked the car near the Tidal Basin and they walked through the parkland that surrounded the National Mall, their footsteps sinking into lush green grass.

Tourists, weary from a day spent tramping past memorials and through museums, were lining up to get back into their buses. A middle-aged man shepherded a procession of tired children past an ice-cream stand.

As Mary and Tom climbed the steps to the imposing

Greek-style building that housed the statue of Abraham Lincoln, she remembered the first time she'd come here with Ed, when Ethan was still a toddler. It had been winter then, and Ethan, wrapped in his thick bundle of warm clothes, had been heavy so Ed had carried him.

She could still picture Ed standing on these steps—blond, blue-eyed and laughing, his cheeks reddened by the cold, with the backdrop of winter-white sky behind him. Later that day he'd proposed to her, but while they'd been here, at the memorial, he'd paid a great deal of attention to the Gettysburg Address, carved into the granite wall—just as Tom was doing now.

'I've wanted to see this for a long time,' Tom told her. 'It's so great that Americans have such an imposing memorial to remind them "that these dead shall not have died in vain".'

She knew he was thinking of Ed.

He's not dead, Tom. We mustn't think that he's gone.

She tried to tell him, but the tension that had been building all day joined forces with a burst of sorrow for Ed and her voice refused to work. Without warning, tears streamed down her face.

Embarrassed, she turned her back on Tom and stared hard in the opposite direction, at the towering white Washington monument and its impressive mirror image in the long Reflecting Pool.

She sensed Tom moving close behind her.

'I'm sorry,' he said softly. 'You still believe that by some miracle Ed's going to walk in your front door, don't you?'

'Can't you understand? I have to believe that. Until there's definite news it would be disloyal to think anything else.'

'I can't imagine how hard it must be for you.'

Something white flapped in her peripheral vision and she realised he was offering her his handkerchief. As she turned he murmured, 'Hold still,' and he dabbed at her cheeks and blotted her tear-splashed eyelashes. Then he folded the handkerchief and offered it to her. 'Do you want to blow your nose?'

'Thanks.'

She blew noisily and then put his handkerchief in her pocket, and they stood on the steps in silence, watching as a family of ducks broke the surface of the Reflecting Pool to chase bread thrown by a little boy.

Tom drew a deep breath and let it out slowly. 'Have dinner with me, Mary.'

'Oh, Tom, I don't think I should.' But it was so hard to ignore the wrench of longing his invitation evoked.

He reached out and took her hand. 'You'd like to, wouldn't you?'

This man was her first love. The man she'd wanted to run away with. The father of her child.

His dark eyes studied her and a silent, inchoate message passed between them. *So many sweet, passionate memories…* She was helpless to hide how she felt.

'I feel so torn,' she said.

'I know, so just this once let me make up your mind for you.'

'All right.'

It was a minor victory but an important one, Tom told himself as they went back to her car. She drove him to a part of town where there were plenty of restaurants to choose from and, because they were only casually dressed, they selected a bistro with tables set outside on the cobbled pavement.

He ordered a hamburger. 'I can't visit America without having a hamburger.'

Mary chose soup and a salad.

'What about some wine?' he asked.

'Thanks, I'd like that.'

'Red or white?'

'You're the one making the decisions tonight, so you choose.' Her eyes reflected the sparkle of the outdoor candle on the tabletop between them and he saw a glimpse of the old Mary, the vivacious twenty-year-old. 'I'm ambidextrous,' she joked. 'I can drink red or white.'

'Terrific,' he said, smiling at her relaxed humour and pleased to see that she was starting to shed some of the stress that had been weighing her down. He made a selection and the waiter left to fetch their wine. 'You know, I'm ambidextrous too.' He held up both hands. 'I mean I'm literally ambidextrous—you know—two hands.'

Her eyes widened. 'You can use your right hand just as easily as your left?'

'Sure can.'

'For writing?'

'For writing, throwing a ball, shooting a weapon. It's a very handy skill for a soldier.'

She seemed upset. 'How come you never told me that before?'

'I don't know. I don't suppose the topic ever came into our conversations before.'

For a moment she sat very still, staring at the candle, then she drew in a long, deep breath. 'This is so hard, Tom—being here, like this, with you again. I'm trying not to think about what might have been.'

'I guess—that's—sensible.'

'We were too young, weren't we?'

'Do you think so?'

At first she didn't answer. Then finally, 'I'd go crazy if I didn't believe that.'

Tom sighed. 'I suppose it's possible that we were too young and naive and carried away with the romance of being in love.'

He offered it as the rational response she wanted, but it felt like a lie, and Mary seemed less pleased with his comment than he'd expected. Her brown eyes looked troubled, shimmering with the threat of more tears.

She shifted restlessly on her chair and forced a bright smile. 'I shouldn't have raised the subject. Let's not talk about it. Tell me some more about your plans for the farm.'

He obliged by telling her about his ideas for marketing Pirelli Tea internationally. Business and marketing were subjects close to her heart, and she grew enthusiastic as they thrashed out the pros and cons of possible website designs and strategies for expanding the Pirelli Tea Company.

'I'll have to send you my recipe for spiced Chai tea,' she said. 'It's the hot new item in American cafés. If you add it to your range of teas in Australia it could be a big hit.'

By the time their meals arrived they were chatting easily. And as the wine relaxed them both they spoke no more of the past. But afterwards, as they walked back beneath leafy elms, Tom took her hand—just for old times' sake, he told himself. And Mary let him hold it until they reached her car, which was parked in a quiet side street.

When she tried to pull her hand from his he tightened his grip. 'Not so fast,' he murmured.

Her face was in shadows but a street light, filtered by

the overhead branches, picked out the smooth whiteness of her throat. He moved closer.

'Tom—' she whispered.

'Shh. Remember, you're letting me make the decisions tonight.' He drew her closer. God, he wanted to kiss her. His Mary.

Every cell in his body urged him to tip her chin upwards so that her mouth could meet his. Her lips would be exquisitely soft and would taste of the strawberries they'd eaten for dessert. At the very least he needed to kiss the sweet, slender curve of her neck.

But he could feel the tension building in her again. And while he hesitated she moved away, with just the slightest twist of her head sideways.

'O-o-oh.'

Her soft moan came on a trembling breath. She looked up and Tom saw in her lovely brown eyes a harrowing message of loss and regret, and he felt as if his heartstrings had been ripped from his chest.

Then she pulled away quickly. 'I'll take you back to your hotel,' she said.

Their conversation lapsed into uncomfortable silence on the short journey back to the hotel. As Mary pulled over to the kerbside she asked, 'When are you leaving?'

'I have a plane booked for Monday morning.'

She nodded slowly, then looked at him, her brown eyes soft and shimmering. 'Did you make a special trip to the States just to bring the watch for Ethan?'

'Yes,' he said.

'That's so good of you.'

'It was the least I could do.'

'Thank you, Tom.' She almost reached out to touch him, but just in time she resisted, and curled her hand into a fist on her lap instead. 'There's so much I have to thank you for. For being such a good friend to Ed. And for Ethan's castle. For dinner tonight. And—and thank you for understanding—about everything—'

'Hold it,' Tom cut in. His face was grim and dark as he unsnapped his seat belt and reached for the door handle. 'Don't assume too much.' In one swift, slick movement he pushed the door open and leapt out of the car.

Sick at heart, Mary watched through the windscreen as he skirted around the front of her car to the pavement. Beside her again, he bent down and tapped on her window. Her heartbeat grew more erratic as she depressed the button to lower it.

'There are limits to my understanding,' he said crisply. 'Don't ever imagine it's been a picnic for me to come here—to find you after all this time—married to another man. Mother to another man's son.'

Then he straightened abruptly, turned, and strode into the hotel without looking back.

CHAPTER SEVEN

IT WAS tearing her apart.

Mary tossed and turned, unable to sleep, torn by guilt and desire, hope and sorrow.

For five and a half years she'd been Mary Cameron McBride, a devoted Army wife who dedicated herself to her husband and son.

But Tom, the father of her son, had walked back into her life and shown her with startling clarity that circumstances, her cousin and her father had interfered with her destiny.

Tom was her destiny. When she was twenty she'd been absolutely certain that she'd been born to love Tom—and only Tom. Now she was learning all over again that his hold on her heart was inescapable.

His parting words had shaken her. She'd driven home with tears streaming down her face, knowing that her passion for him had never died.

But where did that leave Ed?

Poor Ed. Her good and honest husband.

To deny her feelings for Tom felt dishonest, but to acknowledge them felt disloyal to Ed. What could she do?

It was so difficult to accept Tom's assurance that Ed had died. But Tom had been there at the scene of the accident. He was an experienced Special Operative. And he was a realist.

She, on the other hand, had been clinging to a vain hope that there'd been a terrible mistake, that the Army had simply lost track of Ed, and that any day now he would sail in through her front door with his wide grin and his kind, twinkling blue eyes and her life would settle back into place.

Tom was quite certain that was impossible.

Now, as moonlight streamed through her bedroom window, she stared at Ed's smiling face in the photograph on the dressing table beside her.

She'd known when they married that it had been a compromise for both of them. Ed had told her that there had been a young woman in his past whom he might have married if he'd been fertile, but he hadn't wanted to deny her the joys of motherhood.

And Ed knew that Mary had loved Ethan's father. But by tacit agreement they'd put their pasts behind them.

They'd become man and wife, and if their love was based more on friendship and mutual respect than passion it wasn't any less real.

But her love for Tom was such a powerful force that it stormed inside her, making her toss and turn as she clutched the white Irish linen handkerchief that he had used to dry her tears. Over and over her fingers traced the navy-blue initial T embroidered in the corner.

She told herself that she was glad she'd resisted Tom's kiss. Except…

Would one kiss have been so wrong? If she'd shared one kiss with him she'd have had something to remember in the long days to come.

She thought about how the kiss might have felt, and longing coiled in the pit of her stomach. If she closed her eyes she could *almost* sense the touch of Tom's mouth on hers.

She could picture it. They'd been together on the footpath—his face dappled by the street light filtering through tree branches. She could see every detail of his face as he leaned to kiss her. His eyes, dark with desire; the sexy bump on his nose where it had been broken. She could sense the rough evening shadow of beard on his jaw and his scrumptious lips coming closer...

Oh, man... Would Tom have kissed her gently?

She tried to imagine his lips brushing sweetly, softly, teasingly over hers, but just at the vital moment of contact the image dissolved.

Perhaps their kiss would have been frenzied and passionate, making the most of that one brief moment. But she couldn't imagine that either.

She tried to remember Tom's kisses from the past, but her mind kept playing tricks so that even they were lost to her.

Whenever she pictured their lips meeting, she kept hearing his parting words: *'Don't ever imagine it's been a picnic for me to come here—to find you after all this time—married to another man. Mother to another man's son.'*

Oh, Tom, if only you knew...

Oh, God, what was the best thing, the right thing, to do? Why couldn't she be wise?

It took for ever for dawn to arrive, and she'd never been so grateful for the first grey light of day. As soon as the sky beyond her window began to pale she crawled out of bed, pulled on faded jeans and a comfy, loose T-shirt and stumbled downstairs into her kitchen to make coffee and drag out recipe books.

Whenever she felt really low she baked. She had no idea where her inclination for comfort-baking came from. It wasn't something she'd learned in her mother's kitchen, and she was more likely to give the results away to others than to eat them, but there was something about measuring and sifting, blending and beating that usually soothed her.

Usually.

But today when she threw herself into baking—peanut butter cookies for Ethan, Frank's favourite apple sauce and raisin cookies and a huge pound cake, so she could offer her father-in-law a hearty afternoon tea when he brought Ethan home—she didn't feel any better.

At the end of her baking frenzy the cookies and cake had turned out perfectly and sat cooling on wire racks while the delicious smell of their baking lingered in her sunny yellow kitchen, she still felt wretched.

Tom was going back to Australia. She would never see him again. He had come back into her life for two short days. How could she bear to let him go again? Once there'd been a time when she'd thought he would be hers for ever.

Curse her father! Curse Sonia! Tom was the man she should have been with all these years.

Shoving mixing bowls roughly into the dishwasher, she filled the sink with hot, sudsy water, seized a scouring pad and attacked the baking tins as if they were her enemy. *Curse the terrorists and their filthy wars!* She'd made peace with herself and she'd made a good life with Ed. And now everything was falling apart.

With angry swipes she polished the benchtops till they shone and, when there was nothing left to clean she marched to the end of her kitchen and stood staring at the telephone.

Should she ring Tom? If she did, what on earth would she say?

He was probably at his hotel—or perhaps he'd already left to make the most of his last chance to see the sights of Washington.

Would she make matters worse if she rang him? It would be cruel to tell a man that she'd never stopped loving him when she was still married to someone else.

And it would be pathetic to tell him that she was eaten hollow by regret because she hadn't let him kiss her last night.

Lost in vexed thoughts, she jumped when the doorbell rang. Next moment a masculine voice called, 'Mary, are you there?'

It sounded like Tom.

In a flash she was flying down the hall and flinging open the door.

It *was* Tom.

Tom on her doorstep, standing in a shaft of morning sunlight.

'Good morning,' he said.

'Hello.'

'I hope you don't mind my calling again.'

'No, of course I don't mind.' She was giddy with joy.

'I want to apologise for the way I spoke when I left you last night,' he said.

'I was about to phone you for much the same reason.'

He looked surprised.

'Would you like to come inside?' she asked, stepping back into the hall.

'Thanks.' He followed her into the house. 'Something smells great. Have you been baking?'

'I thought I might need to bribe Ethan to go to school this week, so I've made some tempting goodies for his lunchbox.'

'Lucky Ethan.'

Her nerves kicked in as she led him into the lounge. She caught sight of her reflection in the mirror over the fireplace and saw that limp strands of her hair had straggled out of the tortoiseshell clip she'd used to keep her hair up while she baked. As for her T-shirt—good grief, there were streaks of flour and cocoa. She looked a mess.

To make up for her shabby appearance, she became suddenly formal. 'Would you like some morning tea?'

'No, thank you,' he said politely.

He stood in the middle of the Turkish rug, stealing her breath because he looked sensational even though he was dressed in ordinary blue jeans and a dark blue shirt. His hair was wonderfully shiny and black and his eyes were as dark as black coffee. It was so good to see him. She wanted to look and look.

She opened her mouth to offer him a seat, but before she could speak he said, 'I'm sorry about the way I barked at you last night.'

'You don't need to apologise.'

'I do. It's important.' He frowned. 'And there's something else.' Hitching a hand on his hip, he lifted the other to rub the back of his neck. 'I'm afraid what I'm going to say next isn't going to make life any easier for you, Mary, but I have to say it.'

Her heart began to thump.

Tom drew a deep breath and expelled it quickly as he dropped his hands back to his sides. 'Ed and I were good mates. I really loved the guy—but you do understand that he's not coming back, don't you? No one could have survived that drop.'

A painful lump dammed her throat. 'I'm beginning to realise that it must be true.'

'It is true, Mary. I believe it, and I wouldn't say what I'm going to say next if I didn't.'

She gulped and nodded.

'It's just that— I can't leave here without letting you know how much you still mean to me.'

A shocked thrill flashed through her—the sort of thrill a dancer must feel when she's tossed into the air and left to hope that her partner would catch her.

Tom kept talking quickly. 'I can't pretend that I've been pining for you for the past eight years. In fact I was confident that I'd managed to put the idea of you out of my mind. But—'

He smiled a beautiful, slow, sad smile. 'Either a part of you stayed with me, or you took a part of me with you. I'm not sure which way it happened. But, now that I'm seeing you again, I realise that I've never been completely free of you.' He took a step towards her.

'It's—it's like that for me, too, Tom.'

For long seconds they stood there, staring at each other, their eyes sending messages that added weight to their words. Mary felt aglow, as if someone had lit a string of party lights inside her.

'I felt so bad about sending you back to Australia without explaining how I felt,' she said. 'But I didn't know how to start. It's all so complicated. I feel dreadful about hurting you, and I feel bad about Ed, and then I feel guilty for wanting you. I can't think what's right.'

He smiled again. 'Mary-Mary quite contrary.' After a pause he added, 'Actually, I'm just as bad. I've been driving myself nuts all night.'

Reaching out, he touched her cheek. His dark eyes shimmered as he let his thumb trail over her skin, skimming close to her lips. For one tantalising moment she thought he was going to kiss her, and she felt a swift, sharp flash of anticipation.

Her lips parted.

But then, with an anguished sigh, Tom dropped his hand and took one step back from her. 'I promised myself that I wouldn't put any kind of pressure on you. That I would tell you how I felt and then leave.'

What could she say? She knew she should be grateful for his restraint. If Tom had kissed her she might have lost her head—just as she had when she was young. She supposed she *was* grateful. The strength of her feelings scared her. She was still married, or at the least newly widowed, and yet she was feverish with longing for Tom Pirelli.

Thank heavens he had enough self-control for both of them.

Following his lead, she too took a step back, and she crossed her arms, hugging them tight against her chest. 'Thank you for understanding, Tom. At the moment, until things are—clearer…until I hear something definite about Ed… I feel as if someone's pressed a pause button on my life.'

His eyes surveyed her bleakly. 'That's fair enough.'

Fair? Was she really being fair? Guilt gripped her once more as she thought of her dark secret. More than ever Tom deserved to know about his son, and if there was a way to make the news pleasing she might have told him. But chances were he'd be dreadfully upset. From his point of view he'd been cheated of his rights, and that was a terrible blow to inflict on a man on the eve of his departure. Tom was a soldier going home from battle. He needed to return to his family with his heart set on peace and hope.

I promise I'll tell you, Tom, just as soon as we know something definite. As soon as word comes through…

With forced brightness, she changed the subject. 'I think it's time that I made you some of my spiced Chai tea.'

His mouth pulled into a wry grin. 'Chai tea. Great.'

'Let me fix you something to eat. It's not too early for lunch, is it? I have some cold chicken. I'll make a chicken sandwich, and *then* you can have Chai tea with a big slice of pound cake.'

'That sounds a hell of a lot safer than what I was thinking about.'

It was a beautiful clear summer's day, without being too hot, so they ate on the back deck. Mary laid a yellow gingham cloth over the white cane table and set it with her favourite blue and white china. And she took a moment to flee upstairs to swap her daggy old T-shirt for a fresh pale pink linen blouse, and to brush her hair and dash a tawny pink gloss over her lips.

Although Tom didn't comment on the changes, she could sense his approval. And she sensed it again as they sat outside to eat their sandwiches. He kept casting admiring glances over her garden. She was rather proud of her bright summer display. She'd planted begonias, impatiens and dianthus in beds that bordered the deck, and she'd filled three hanging baskets with deep purple and white petunias that looked stunning combined with red and gold coleus and cool green ivy.

'The Mary, Mary of nursery rhyme fame was good at gardening, wasn't she?' he said.

She suspected he was teasing her, but he redeemed himself when he added, 'You know, you've made this standard Army issue place into a very lovely home.'

She found herself mumbling, 'Thanks.' And then, overcome by a need to banish wistful thoughts about the home she might have shared with him, she asked, 'So what do you think of your Chai tea?'

He took a sip from the big blue and white cup and pulled a face. 'It's OK. There's a bit too much cinnamon and spice for my taste, but I can see it's the kind of thing chicks would go for.'

'You'd better believe it. You should add it to your repertoire if you're planning a range of gourmet specialties.'

He shrugged, yet to be convinced. 'Now, this pound cake is a different matter.' He broke off a generous piece. 'This I could go for in a big way. If my dad tasted it he would want to set you up in a little teahouse in Millaa Millaa, selling Tableland tea and coffee and homemade cakes to the tourists.'

'That would be fun.'

He grinned. 'He's always wanted to buy a little café and call it *Pirelli's*.'

She tried to ignore the way her spirits swooped when she thought of him settling back home in North Queensland, building a new life. Would she ever be able to join him there?

What would have happened if they had married? Would she and Tom have been living on his tea plantation? She might have been running the café his father dreamed about—a cute little timber cottage with a long view down a misty valley. The cottage would be painted green and white and turned into a teahouse, with colourful pot plants and hanging baskets gracing the front veranda.

'You get a lot of tourists up on the Tablelands, don't you?' she asked him.

'Sure. In summer everyone flocks there to get away from the heat, and in winter they come to cosy up in front of a fireplace.'

Heaven help her. She couldn't stop thinking about what might have been. Ethan would have been living there too. She could picture him running about happily on Tom's plantation, exploring a fern-fringed creek for platypus, or running over long, sloping green fields with a frisky dog at his heels. Her son would have grown up with his real grandparents and his sweet old Italian great-grandmother with her dark coffee eyes—just like his.

'How are your parents?' Tom asked, bringing her back with a jolt.

Alarmed by the wayward direction of her thoughts, she sat forward quickly, picking up her teacup and nursing it in both hands. 'My parents are both well, but—they're not together any more.'

He frowned. 'You mean they've split up? Divorced?'

'Yes. Mum left Dad when they went back to Australia.'

'Was that a surprise?'

'Yes it was—although I realised later that there had been hints. Mum never actually came out and said as much, but I don't think she ever forgave my father for the way he—' She broke off, shocked that she'd almost mentioned her pregnancy. 'She'd had enough of being bossed around by him.'

'So where are they now?'

'States apart. As soon as Mum set foot on Australian soil she took off and found herself a dear little bluestone house in Adelaide, and now she has a lovely new husband and is very happy.'

'And your father?'

'Retired from the Army and owner of a caravan park in northern New South Wales. I'm afraid he's set up a million rules and runs it as if he's Park Commandant.'

'And I guess you stayed here because you were already married to Ed?' Tom said.

That wasn't quite the way it had happened. In reality, her parents' return to Australia had prompted Ed's proposal. But she couldn't tell Tom any part of that without revealing that her marriage had come after her pregnancy and not before. Once again her stomach churned guiltily.

Tom leaned back in his chair and looked up at the sky, staring at the white vapour trail left by a jet, then he cleared his throat and leaned forward again, resting his elbows on the table. 'Mary, this situation we've found ourselves in... I know you have a great deal to think about. Not just about Ed, there's Ethan and Ed's parents.'

'Yes,' she whispered, her heart thrumming.

He reached out across the table and her skin flashed heat as his fingers caressed her cheek once more. 'Can I ask you to remember a couple of things while you're trying to sort it all out?'

His voice, his eyes and his caress sent her heartbeat scampering madly. Pressing her cheek against the curve of his hand, she asked, 'What do you want me to remember?'

'I'm alive. I'm not going to fight any more wars and I love you, Mary.'

She couldn't answer. Tears threatened and she didn't want to spoil things by crying. Turning her face, she pressed a kiss into his hand. She swallowed hard, trying to suppress the sobs forming in her throat.

'Mary,' Tom whispered. He rounded the table and was at her side, drawing her out of her chair, clasping her hand against his chest. Then, without a word, he led her across the deck and into the privacy of the lounge, where he hauled her against him. 'You know there's going to be a time in the future when you are free?'

She nodded against his shoulder.

'And I'm going to claim you.' His arms tightened around her.

Again she nodded, her heart too full for words.

She felt his lips in her hair, then brushing her brow. Helpless with longing, she let her head tip back so that her face was raised to his.

'Mary, I can't leave here without one kiss,' he whispered.

Her skin burned and Tom looked at her with such heartbreaking tenderness that she trembled. And he was trembling too. She could feel it in his hands as they cupped her face. And then his lips touched hers.

And... *Ah, yes!*

This was what Tom's kiss felt like. This magic meeting of lips. Soft, yet strong. Setting her alight with their very first contact. This aching, soul-searing, sweeping pressure. This warm mingling of mouths.

She was his. Her lips were begging him to seek and claim her. Tom. Her Tom.

His arms pulled her in till there was nothing between them, and she wound her arms around his neck, drinking in the remembered taste of him, the special smell of his skin, the sensuous thrill of his tongue deep inside her.

Everything she had ever felt for Tom was back in full force. Her body turned to liquid fire as his taut, toned length pushed hard against her, as they strained together, letting the combined force of their passion pour over and through them.

No kiss had ever felt so necessary or so right. Deep, impassioned, it was a kiss that reached into her soul, demanding never to be forgotten. It was as if she and Tom were part of some grand celestial plan beyond their imagining. He was the father of her son, and he was the man she loved, had always loved.

They found ways to make the kiss last, changing angles, varying tempo and rhythm—not wanting to ever separate. Was it possible for one kiss to say everything, be everything?

Mary clung to him, knowing that this was goodbye. Tomorrow he would be returning to Australia, too soon… They broke apart and gazed breathlessly into each other's eyes.

'Ever since I saw you on Friday I've been thinking about this,' Tom confessed.

'So have I.'

He dropped a kiss on her forehead. 'Perhaps I should go now, while I'm ahead.' He smiled as if to lighten the moment.

'I don't want you to go,' she whispered. Then, with a sigh, she drew back. 'But I know it would be sensible for you to go now.'

'Can I use your phone to call for a taxi?'

'Of course.'

He turned and, with his arm around her shoulders, they walked through the house to the kitchen. After he'd made the phone call he said, 'I'll ring you tonight.'

'It might be best if I ring you. I'll wait till Ethan's asleep. It should be shortly after eight.' She forced a brave smile. 'And then you should sleep. It's such a long flight back.'

He nodded and said somewhat irrelevantly, 'It'll be winter at home.'

'Your family will be so pleased to see you.'

'Yes, it's been a long time since I had leave.'

'I'm so glad you came here today, Tom.'

'So am I, Mary-Mary. So am I.'

There was the sound of a car at the front of the house.

'Is that the taxi already?' She hurried to a window to look out to the street. 'Oh, it's Frank with Ethan.' She glanced towards Tom.

Scooping her close, he whispered, 'Don't forget you're going to be mine.'

'I promise, Tom. I love you.'

Tingling with secret joy, they separated and walked down the hallway to the front door. There was a patter of footsteps on the front porch and an impatient trill from the doorbell.

'Mum, are you there?'

'Yes, I'm here,' Mary cried, opening the door and holding her arms for her son's hug. Bursting with emotion, she squeezed him extra hard. Over his shoulder she smiled at Frank and hoped there was nothing about her face or manner that showed she'd just been thoroughly kissed. 'Hi, Frank. Have you had a good day?'

'We've had a grand day,' Frank cried heartily. Then he saw Tom standing behind her and his eyebrows lifted. 'Hi, Tom.' He didn't quite manage to keep the wariness from his voice.

An anxious knot tightened in Mary's stomach as she realised that Susan must have spoken to Frank; he knew that Tom was Ethan's father.

'I just came to say goodbye,' Tom said. 'I'm heading for home in the morning.'

Frank nodded and held out his hand to shake Tom's. 'I hope you have a safe journey.' With an uncharacteristic steely glint in his eyes, he added, 'And thanks for bringing that watch back to us. It'll mean a lot to Ethan when he's older.'

To Mary's relief, the taxi arrived then. She and Tom exchanged polite goodbyes and a brief handshake.

Tom held out his hand to Ethan and the boy shook it shyly. 'Keep that castle well defended,' Tom told him.

'Yes, sir.'

Then he loped down the steps two at a time, hurried down the front path and disappeared inside the taxi.

The trio on the porch waved, and as the taxi rounded the corner they went into the house.

CHAPTER EIGHT

'NONNA?' Tom smiled as he spoke into the hotel phone.

'Yes, who is it?'

'It's Tom, Nonna. How are you?'

'Oh, Toto, dear boy, I'm wonderful. Where are you?'

'I'm in America. In Washington DC. I didn't wake you up, did I?'

'No, you know we get up with the sun. It's so good to hear your voice.'

'You'll hear a lot more of it soon. I'm coming home. I'll be home in two days.'

'Two days? That's such good news. I'll get your father. He's having his breakfast.'

'Don't disturb him, Nonna. Let me talk to you.'

'All right then. Now, tell me—are you fit and well? Are they feeding you good food?'

'I'm in perfect health. How's everyone at home?'

'We're all doing OK. Hey, Toto, you sound good. You sound happy.'

'I am happy, Nonna.'

'You're in love!'

Chuckling, he flopped back on to the hotel bed and grinned up at the ceiling. 'How'd you guess?'

'I'm your nonna, I can hear it in your voice. Tell me about her. She's beautiful, isn't she?'

'Of course.'

'Where does she live?'

'Here. In America.'

An Important Message from the Editors

Dear Reader,

If you'd enjoy reading romance novels with larger print that's easier on your eyes, let us send you TWO FREE HARLEQUIN ROMANCE® NOVELS in our LARGER PRINT EDITION. These books are complete and unabridged, but the type is set about 20% bigger to make it easier to read. Look inside for an actual-size sample.

By the way, you'll also get a surprise gift with your two free books!

Pam Powers

Peel off Seal and Place Inside...

FREE BOOKS

THE RIGHT WOMAN

she'd thought she was fine. It took Daniel's words and Brooke's question to make her realize she was far from a full recovery.

She'd made a start with her sister's help and she intended to go forward now. Sarah felt as if she'd been living in a darkened room and some-one had suddenly opened a door, letting in the fresh air and sunshine. She could feel its warmth slowly seeping into the coldest part of her. The feeling was liberating. She realized it was only a small step and she had a long way to go, but she was ready to face life again with Serena and her family behind her.

All too soon, they were saying goodbye and Sarah experienced a moment of sadness for all the years she and Serena had missed. But they d each other now and that's what

She held asy

Printed in the U.S.A.
Publisher acknowledges the copyright holder of the excerpt from this individual work as follows:
THE RIGHT WOMAN Copyright © 2004 by Linda Warren. All rights reserved.
® and ™ are trademarks owned and used by the trademark owner and/or its licensee.

YOURS FREE!
You'll get a great mystery gift with your two free larger print books!

GET TWO FREE LARGER PRINT BOOKS!

YES! Please send me two free Harlequin Romance® novels in the larger print edition, and my free mystery gift, too. I understand that I am under no obligation to purchase anything, as explained on the back of this insert.

PLACE FREE GIFTS SEAL HERE

119 HDL EFWH   319 HDL EFWT

FIRST NAME	LAST NAME

ADDRESS

APT.#	CITY

STATE / PROV.	ZIP/POSTAL CODE

Are you a current Harlequin Romance® subscriber and want to receive the larger print edition?
Call 1-800-221-5011 today!

◄ **DETACH AND MAIL CARD TODAY!** ►

(H-RLPR-03/06) © 2004 Harlequin Enterprises Ltd.

The Harlequin Reader Service™ — Here's How It Works:

Accepting your 2 free Harlequin Romance® larger print books and gift places you under no obligation to buy anything. You may keep the books and gift and return the shipping statement marked "cancel." If you do not cancel, about a month later we'll send you 4 additional Harlequin Romance larger print books and bill you just $3.82 each in the U.S., or $4.30 each in Canada, plus 25¢ shipping & handling per book and applicable taxes if any.* That's the complete price and — compared to cover prices of $4.50 each in the U.S. and $5.25 each in Canada — it's quite a bargain! You may cancel at any time, but if you choose to continue, every month we'll send you 4 more books, which you may either purchase at the discount price or return to us and cancel your subscription.

*Terms and prices subject to change without notice. Sales tax applicable in N.Y. Canadian residents will be charged applicable provincial taxes and GST.

'Oh. That's not such good news. What are you going to do about it?'

'It's OK. I'll work it out.' Suddenly he swung upright again and clutched the phone. 'Nonna, you might as well know. I've found Mary.'

This was greeted by silence, then, 'Mary? That girl who broke your heart?'

'Yes.'

'Oh, Toto. Do you know what you're doing?'

'Yes, I've never been surer.'

'Is she coming back with you?'

'Not yet. I'll explain the whole story when I get home, but don't you worry about me. It's going to be fine, just fine, Nonna.'

'OK, I believe you for now. But you hurry home. I want to look into your face and see for myself that this Mary is making you happy.'

'OK. I'll see you very soon. Behave yourself until Tuesday—no, it'll be Wednesday your time before I get home. *Ciao.*'

'Have a safe journey, Toto. *Ciao.*'

Tom told himself that a man aged thirty shouldn't get so worked up about a kiss. But the truth of it was that although he'd dated his share of women in the past eight years a simple kiss from Mary had eclipsed all the rest.

From the first trembling touch of Mary's lips he'd been lost. Lost in the delicate, unforgettable taste of her. Driven wild by the sensational smoothness of her skin beneath his hands, by the sexy pressure of her sweet breasts straining against him, the soft, eager little sounds she made as her excitement mounted.

He had been spellbound by the same mysterious magic and amazing chemistry of their youth. With Mary in his arms again, he was a born again convert to the reality of love. Love was real! It was powerful. It made sense of life.

Nothing could dim his happiness—not even the fact that Mary was Ed's wife.

He felt no guilt about kissing Mary. There wasn't the slightest pang that he'd done anything to be ashamed of. If he'd thought Ed could ever know, or be hurt by his actions, he would have stayed clear away. But Tom was certain that Ed couldn't be hurt…

This was Mary. *His* Mary. And now that he knew the truth about how they'd been cheated out of marriage he felt as if she'd always been his. They deserved this second chance at happiness.

He strolled down to a local bistro to eat an early evening meal and, back in his hotel room afterwards, whistled happily off-key as he showered and changed into boxer shorts and a T-shirt.

Eyeing the mini-bar, he decided to have a beer. It wasn't quite time for Mary to ring yet, so he pressed the remote control for the television and, beer in one hand, remote in the other, stretched back on the quilted bedspread to do a little channel-surfing.

He deliberately avoided the news and anything grim and flicked through about forty channels, searching for something light.

Mary was taking ages to call, but Tom didn't worry. He whiled away the time by thinking about her—imagining her putting Ethan to bed. She would be the kind of mother who made sure her son cleaned his teeth properly and then she would read him bedtime stories. He pictured her with Ethan, their blonde heads close together in a lamp's light while she read to him in her lovely soft blend of Australian-American accents.

She would tuck Ethan into bed with a hug and a kiss. *Did the kid have any idea how lucky he was?*

Half an hour passed and he grew more restless. Striding to the window, he looked out across the vista of Washington DC. The purple haze of summer twilight had almost given way to the velvet-black of night. Street lights, the interior lights of buildings and the headlights of traffic glowed and shimmered across the dignified city.

Somewhere out there Mary was being kept busy, while he prowled a hotel room like a caged beast. After three-quarters of an hour he could bear it no longer. He dialled her number.

'Hello?'

Her voice sounded tiny, querulous, distant.

'Hi, Mary. Is Ethan in bed yet?'

'No.'

That single word sounded like a sob. Hairs rose on the back of Tom's neck. 'What's the matter? You sound upset.'

'I've had a call from the Army, Tom. The most amazing thing's happened.'

'What?'

'Ed's coming home.'

CHAPTER NINE

'WHAT?'

'Ed's alive, Tom. They're bringing him back. He's on his way now and should arrive at Walter Reed Army Hospital some time tomorrow.'

'My God, that's—that's great news.' Tom was thrilled for Ed. Of course he was. But he was appalled by his own equally strong dismay. 'It's amazing.'

'I know. I can't believe it.'

'Did they say anything about his condition?'

'He's in bad shape. I think his condition is critical. I haven't been given many details yet, but I guess he'll need to be in hospital for quite some time.'

'Right.' Sweat broke on Tom's brow.

'I've rung Ed's parents,' said Mary. 'They're coming back to DC tonight, so they'll be ready and waiting when he arrives.'

'They'll stay with you?'

'I offered, but they rang the hospital and were told that there's accommodation for families close by Walter Reed. Susan's beside herself. She's so happy.'

'I suppose she is.' Tom, on the other hand, and to his eternal shame, could feel nothing but alarm. 'What about you, Mary?'

'I'll stay here. It's not that far across town.'

'I meant how are you feeling?'

'Oh, I don't know. I—I feel kind of numb. I think I'm in shock.'

'Yeah, I guess you must be. Don't forget to take care of yourself. What about Ethan? I suppose he's excited.'

'He is.' He heard her deep sigh. 'I've tried to explain to him that his daddy is still very sick.'

'Is there anything I can do?'

'Oh, Tom, I don't know.' Without warning, she burst into a flood of tears.

'Mary,' Tom called, raising his voice, 'can you hear me? I'm going to come over.'

But the tears had taken hold of her. There was no answer except loud, uncontrollable sobbing. Tom swallowed and blinked. 'Can you hear me, Mary? Hold on. I'm coming.'

Finally she mumbled something incomprehensible and disconnected.

Tom replaced the receiver, sank on to the edge of the bed and covered his face with his hands. No matter how hard he tried to fight it, one thought kept pushing all others aside.

He was going to lose Mary. *Again.*

He couldn't bear it. To lose her felt like death.

Why couldn't he have been the one to fall from that damn chopper, instead of Ed? That would have made things easier for everyone. Ed would be home safe and sound with his wife and son, and he and Mary would have been spared any emotional anguish.

As it was, he'd made a complete hash of things. He'd been so damn sure that Ed couldn't have survived that fall, and as a result he'd misled everyone, including himself. Why hadn't he realised that if anyone could pull off a miracle it would be his son-of-a-gun buddy, Ed McBride?

Instead he'd gone to Mary and spilled his heart out, kissed her as if there were no tomorrow, restaked his claim on her future and turned her life upside down, inside out.

Now she would have to take back her promise to love him. Ed was alive. Her husband was coming home. And Tom wasn't sure he had the moral fortitude to be glad.

A terrible, agonised kind of sob broke from his chest. The sound of it horrified him, shocking him into action. He leapt to his feet and reached for the telephone once more.

Fifteen minutes later he sat, tense as a sentry guard, as a taxi whisked him back across the Potomac River to Arlington.

At Mary's house lights glowed in all the downstairs windows. She opened the door to his knock, looking very slender and vulnerable, silhouetted by the brightly lit hallway.

As he stepped closer he saw that her face was now free of tears, but she looked very pale and strained. Still lovely. He had to fight back a fierce desire to haul her into his arms.

'Have you heard any more news?' he asked.

She shook her head.

'I hope you don't mind my coming.' She didn't respond immediately and he rushed on to say, 'You sounded so upset. I had to make sure you were OK.'

'Thanks.'

Tom searched her face anxiously, trying to gauge her mood. He knew she must be happy and relieved about Ed. Her tears would have been reaction—emotional overload from the impact of sudden, unexpected news.

The tight, closed expression in her eyes and mouth told him that she didn't share his sense of desolation—of paradise regained and lost in one short afternoon.

'You'd better come in,' she said.

They went through to the family room off the kitchen. Ethan was lying on a brightly coloured beanbag, watching a cartoon on television. Dressed in striped pyjamas, and with his hair still damp, he had the clean, scrubbed glow that youngsters seemed to acquire when they'd had a warm bath.

To Tom's surprise, the boy greeted him like an old friend. 'Has Mummy told you about my dad?'

'She has,' Tom said. 'It's great news.'

Mary said, 'Take a seat, Tom.' She gestured to one end of a deep cornflower-blue sofa. 'Would you like a drink? I have some wine, or there's Scotch. Or would you prefer coffee?'

'I don't need anything—unless you'd like a drink.'

'I think I might need one tonight. I'll have a glass of wine.'

'Then I'll join you. Let me get it. I can find my way around a kitchen and a bottle opener.'

'No, it's OK. Stay here.' She seemed pleased to be able to hurry away from him into the kitchen.

Tom glanced at his watch. It was after nine. 'Are you staying up late tonight, sport?' he asked Ethan.

The boy shrugged and looked sheepish. 'Mummy wants me to go to bed, but I don't want to go yet.'

'Don't you?'

'Nope.'

'I figured a smart kid like you would be aiming to get big and strong like the Army Rangers.'

'I am.' Ethan's lower lip pushed forward into a pout. 'But that doesn't mean I have to go to bed.'

Tom pretended horror. 'Yes, it does.'

'Why?'

'Don't you know?'

'Know what?'

'I can't believe you don't know.'

Ethan scrambled off his beanbag and hurried across the room towards him. 'What don't I know?'

Tom frowned and shook his head. 'This is serious.'

'Tell me,' Ethan begged.

'I thought all smart boys knew they do their best growing at night time, while they're asleep.'

'Do they?'

'Sure. It's a proven fact. If you stay up late you'll end up puny.'

'What's puny?'

'Pint-sized. The size you are now.'

'I won't get any bigger?'

'Not a chance,' Tom said, shaking his head solemnly.

Ethan's dark eyes narrowed suspiciously. 'I don't believe you. If that was true, my mummy would have told me.'

'Your mummy mightn't know. She's a girl, and girls don't know all the important stuff. Some of it's secret men's business.'

'Oh.' Ethan was clearly impressed. 'Do they tell you that stuff in the Army?'

'They sure do.' Tom stood, maximising his height and squaring his shoulders. 'So, what do you reckon, mate? Time for bed?'

The boy's eyes grew huge, as if Tom had morphed into something as big as the Incredible Hulk. 'Yes.'

'And if you get to sleep quickly,' Tom added, 'you'll make tomorrow come faster.'

'My dad's coming back tomorrow.'

'That's right.'

There was a clink of glass and Tom turned to see Mary coming into the room with a wine bottle and two glasses.

'What's going on?' she asked warily.

'I'm going to bed,' announced Ethan.

'Really?' She didn't try to hide her surprise.

'Tom 'splained about the secret.'

'What secret?' She looked so stricken Tom thought she might faint.

'I've just explained that boys need plenty of sleep if they want to grow big and strong,' he told her, keeping his face deadpan.

'Oh,' she said. 'Well—that's—that's great. I'll just pour Tom a drink and then I'll come and tuck you in, Ethan.'

Ethan looked towards Tom. 'Do you want to see my bedroom? Mummy let me set up my castle in the corner of my room. It looks cool.'

'Sure,' Tom said. 'Is that OK with you, Mary? I'll take him up to bed if you like.'

She opened her mouth to say something and then shut it again. 'That's fine. Come and give me a kiss, little man.'

The boy obliged and Mary watched in amazement as he took Tom's hand, meek as a lamb, and together they climbed the stairs. 'There's a light at the top of the stairs on the right,' she called after them.

Then she set the bottle and glasses on the coffee table and had to sit down quickly, because her legs were shaking so badly she feared she might fall over.

Coming hot on the heels of the incredible news about Ed, this last shock was almost too much. When Ethan had spoken of a secret she'd almost dropped her bundle. For a fraught moment she'd thought that somehow Tom knew about Ethan.

And now she was watching her son and Tom, trotting upstairs to bed, looking so much like father and son...

Oh, God, I don't think I can take much more.

Her hand trembled as she poured herself a drink and took a sip. She'd been stunned by the news that Ed was coming home. She hadn't believed it at first. It had almost been as if someone were playing a terrible joke on her.

She had only just come around to accepting that Ed must be dead, and to allowing herself a glimpse of a new future with Tom. Her afternoon with Tom had made her so happy, and when the news that Ed was coming home had sunk in her first thought had been that she would never see Tom again.

And then, of course, she had felt guilty. How could she be thinking about herself when Ed was going through such a dreadful ordeal? His injuries must be horrific. She could not for one moment question her need to stay with him and do everything in her power to see that he recovered.

But Tom…? Heaven help her, she was going to miss Tom. She didn't know if she could bear the thought of losing him again. If only she could clone herself and leave one dutiful Mary with Ed while the other passionate Mary ran away to pursue happiness with Tom.

Oh, good grief, that was a terrible thought.

It was time to stop thinking.

She was grateful that Tom was upstairs, dealing with Ethan; she'd reached the point where she felt incapable of handling even the smallest problem.

Her mind had been whirling ever since Tom had arrived on Friday, and she didn't want to think any more. If she didn't stop thinking her mind might snap under the weight of it all. It was too much. Trying to think about Ed, Tom, Ed's parents and Ethan…

She sipped some more wine and, leaning back against

the generously upholstered sofa, curled her feet under her, closed her eyes and sighed deeply. Lord, she was tired. She hadn't slept at all last night, and today had been such an emotional rollercoaster. The tears she'd shed after speaking to Tom on the phone had drained her completely.

Now she was utterly exhausted...

When Tom came downstairs he saw at once that Mary was asleep. She was curled on the sofa, her legs tucked beneath her, her head lolling sideways. Her hair spilled over the padded arm of the sofa and it glowed in the lamplight like the delicate gold of angels' wings in medieval paintings.

A granite-hard lump wedged in his throat. When her eyes were closed she looked so much like her little son. They both had the same shiny blonde hair, the same long dark lashes and high cheekbones, the same vulnerable soft pink mouths.

When he bent to remove the almost empty wine glass from her hand she didn't stir, so he took the bottle and glasses through to the kitchen, recorked the bottle and returned it to the refrigerator.

Not wanting to wake her, he went back upstairs to find a pillow and a rug to cover her. He tried the room next to Ethan's first, but it was her study. For a moment he paused, picturing her at work in this room.

It had a very worker-friendly ambience. In the daytime there would be plenty of light flooding from the tall window at the back. Natural features abounded—pot plants, blond timber bookshelves, a huge cork-board covered with notices, clippings, photographs and designs, and an assortment of river-washed stones serving as paperweights on her desk.

The screensaver on her computer showed a scene from

an Australian rainforest—tall timbers, lush palms and ferns, a trickling creek with a stone bridge and, beneath it, moss-covered stones.

About to leave, Tom glanced back at the screen. The curved stone bridge was familiar. *Yes*, it was the old bridge over Crystal Creek in North Queensland.

He stared at it, his heartbeat thudding as he remembered.

Remembered a Saturday in September when Mary had ridden on the back of his motorbike. He'd taken her up the winding mountain road to Mount Spec. They'd gone over that bridge and continued on to Paluma, and they'd picnicked in a long green field on the mountaintop. They'd lain on a tartan picnic rug and fed each other antipasto and they'd rolled down the long grassy slope together—lovesick kids, laughing, kissing, driving each other wild with wanting, desperate to get somewhere more private.

And it had been on the way home, at Crystal Creek— on the old stone bridge—that they'd decided to be married. On this very bridge they'd hatched their plan to elope.

Mary remembered…

All these years, while she'd been married to Ed, she'd clung to that memory.

His heart felt as if it was tearing itself to shreds. He had to get out of there.

Further down the hallway he found her bedroom and entered it cautiously.

This was a large, tasteful and tidy room, carpeted with a thick white wool rug. A deep bay window on the opposite wall was swathed in romantic soft white drapes. Yellow roses in a blue vase stood on the dressing table and there were touches of blue, lemon and green in the decorative knick-knacks.

The big four-poster bed, sumptuous beneath an heirloom patchwork quilt, sent Tom's stomach churning with sickening jealousy but, with more willpower than he'd thought possible, he squashed thoughts of Mary and Ed in that bed and crossed the room to the closet. A light cotton blanket was folded neatly on a high shelf and he took it, as well as a pillow in a snowy white lace-trimmed pillowcase, then headed back downstairs.

There, he drew Mary's slim legs out along the sofa and made her more comfortable, then tucked the soft blanket around her. She made a soft sighing sound and her mouth fell open to offer him a glimpse of pearly teeth, a moist pink tip of tongue and the lush fullness of her lower lip.

Oh, God, only a few short hours ago that lovely mouth had been passionate and fiery as she'd kissed him and kissed him and *kissed* him.

Now her sweet mouth was lost to him. For ever.

The unfairness of it all lodged like a lead weight in his chest. If only he could crawl on to that sofa beside her and take her in his arms, feel her lissom, lovely curves welcoming him one more time. He would make love to her with poetic sensitivity, with such trembling need and shattering passion that God would part the heavens and look down with a beaming smile to say, Well done, Tom.

Yeah, right, mate. Since when had God condoned adultery?

Leaving one table-lamp lit in the corner of the room, he went through the house, turning the rest of the lights out, and as he did so he tried to shake aside the feeling that the darkness was entering his soul.

In the kitchen again, he called for a taxi and went out to the front porch to wait for it, locking Mary's front door behind him.

Next morning Mary rang him quite early, while he was eating breakfast in his hotel room.

'I just wanted to thank you for last night,' she said.

'No problem,' he answered, gulping down a mouthful of toast.

'I'm sorry I went to sleep.'

'You were worn out.'

'It was very sweet of you to take care of Ethan and to look after me like that.'

'Were you comfortable enough on the sofa?'

'Yes, I slept amazingly well. I should try sleeping on the sofa more often.' After a bit, she said, 'I wasn't sure if I'd catch you before you left. What time's your flight?'

'I've cancelled it.'

'Really?' There was an awkward silence. 'That's a shame. You were so looking forward to going home.'

'Ed's my mate, Mary. Surely you don't expect me to go back to Australia without seeing him?'

'No, I guess not.'

'Do you have any more details about his condition?'

'No. All I've heard is that he's been evacuated from a field hospital and they've sedated him rather heavily for the long flight back. He's supposed to be arriving at Walter Reed around ten o'clock. I don't know whether I'll be able to see him straight away, but I plan to be there, of course.'

'Of course.' Another silence fell and Tom pictured Mary, the devoted wife, rushing to Ed's bedside. He lifted his cooling coffee cup from the tray and took a sip, and as he set the cup down again he asked, 'How are you feeling?'

'I'm OK,' she said. 'A good night's sleep makes a world of difference.'

Tom grimaced and released a deep sigh. What had he expected? Had he really thought Mary would tell him how devastated she was that she was no longer free to love him?

'Tom, I'd better go,' she said. 'There's so much to do.'

'Are you taking Ethan with you to the hospital, or is he going to school?'

'I had a moment of weakness and told him he could stay home from school because it's such an important day, and he's so excited. But now I think I've made a mistake. I'm not sure it's a good idea to take him with me this morning. Hospitals can be such scary places. I think I should wait—at least until after I've seen Ed.'

'Yeah, might be wise. And there could be a lot of waiting involved. He'd get upset.'

'Yes.'

'Do you have someone to mind him?'

'I'll probably ring one of my girlfriends.'

'If it's any help, I could take care of him.'

There was a little gasp of surprise on the other end of the line. 'It's OK, Tom. I don't expect you to babysit. You've already done enough...'

Tom couldn't blame Mary. He'd been surprised to hear himself making the offer. But, now he'd started, he wanted to push the issue. 'I may as well make myself useful. I don't have anything else planned, and Ethan and I are starting to hit it off. He's a great little guy.'

This was met by more silence.

'Mary?'

'Do you think it's wise, Tom?'

'What's unwise about it?'

He heard her fretful sigh. 'He can be difficult at times.'

'Mary, I'm trained to handle terrorists. Trust me.'

'Well… I must admit my friends do have busy schedules, and it's Monday morning, which is rather inconvenient timing…'

'Then consider it settled. I'll be your babysitter. I can practise on Ethan before I have to go home to face my nephew and nieces.'

'Well…thanks, Tom.'

'OK. Seeing I'm going to be here for a few more days, I'll get myself a hire car and I'll be over at your house pronto.'

Susan and Frank McBride were already waiting in the hospital reception area when Mary arrived at a quarter to ten.

There were teary kisses and hugs all round as they greeted each other.

Mary shivered. Outside it had been a warm, humid summer's morning, but inside the hospital the air-conditioning seemed uncomfortably cool. Rubbing her bare arms, she looked around at the immaculate highly polished floors, the careful flower arrangements and the framed portraits of famous military surgeons that hung on the walls, and she wished that this morning could be over.

She was frightened—frightened for Ed, who was critically ill, and frightened for herself, for Ed's parents and especially for Ethan. Were they all strong enough to handle this?

A balding man with a stethoscope around his neck approached them. 'Mrs McBride?'

Susan and Mary both stepped towards him. 'Yes?' they said simultaneously.

'You must be Captain McBride's wife,' he said to Mary.

'Yes, I'm Mary, and these are Ed's parents, Susan and Frank.'

They exchanged polite greetings.

Susan leaned forward with her hands clasped in front of her as if she were praying. 'How is our boy?'

'We haven't finished all the tests we need to run yet.'

'But is he going to be all right?' This came from Mary.

'You have a remarkable husband, Mrs McBride.' The doctor smiled faintly and turned to acknowledge Susan and Frank. 'Your son must come from a strong gene pool. He's survived what appears to have been an incredible physical ordeal. He's obviously suffered great privation, and he's had no proper medical care for all this time.'

'So what kind of injuries does he have?' Mary demanded, needing details.

'There are multiple fractures, as you would expect after his fall, and there are internal injuries as well. And I'm afraid he's suffered from tropical infections. That's not surprising, given how long he spent in the jungle without proper medical aid. It's the infections I'm most concerned about. Sometimes they can leave lasting damage.'

'So when will you know if he'll be all right?' The doctor's hesitation frightened Mary, so she asked quickly, 'Can we see him?'

'You should be able to go through for a short visit very soon.'

'Thank you.'

'But don't expect too much. Remember, Captain McBride is still extremely ill.'

'Yes.'

'Can you tell us what happened to him?' Frank asked.

'I don't know the full story, sir. My main focus is to attend to his medical needs, and they're very urgent needs. You'll be fully briefed by someone nominated by his commanding officer. I do know that he was lucky to have been found by the local militia rather than the terrorists. But the main thing now is to try to pull Captain McBride through this medical crisis.'

'Pull him through?' Susan repeated, clearly appalled. 'He will be all right, won't he?'

'Damn it,' cried Frank. 'He can't have survived to this stage and not pull through. You've got to give us more hope than that, Doctor.'

'Mr McBride, as I said, your son is still dangerously ill, but rest assured he's in the best possible care.'

'Well—yes—of course,' Frank said more graciously. 'We know that, we know. Thanks, Doctor.'

Mary felt numb. Numb and cold and frightened.

Her stomach twisted into agonised knots as she tiptoed into the darkened room and saw Ed. He looked so dreadfully thin. His head had been shaved and his skin was sallow, almost yellow. Tubes and drips were hooked up to him and a nurse stood guard at the head of his bed, monitoring the alarming bank of medical machinery.

'Oh, dear Lord,' Susan whispered behind Mary, and

she turned to see her mother-in-law dissolve into sound-less tears on her husband's shoulder.

'There, there. Shh, don't upset him,' Frank said softly.

Mary's heart was beating like a frightened bird's wings, but she went to the side of the bed. A chair had been placed there, so she sat and took Ed's hand in hers.

His eyes opened slowly and his mouth stretched into a smile. 'Mary.'

'Hi, there, soldier,' she whispered. 'Welcome home.' Leaning forward, she kissed him, and his skin felt cold and dry.

'I made it,' Ed said. 'I was determined to get home.' It took all Mary's willpower not to cry. Ed sounded so brave, but she could see the terrible effort it was taking for him to hang on to his smile. He'd always had such a brilliant, warm smile. The sort of smile that lit up his face and made everyone around him start smiling too.

Once he'd told her his motto: *If your face wants to smile, let it; if it doesn't, then make it.*

Now he looked too tired to keep trying, and his hand in hers felt frighteningly thin and frail.

'Who's that?' he asked, trying to focus behind her to his parents.

'It's us, darling,' said his mother, drawing closer. She leant across the bed to kiss his cheek. 'How are you feeling?'

'I'm OK, Mom. Good to see you.'

A sob burst from Susan.

'Come on now, Susan,' said Frank.

'Yeah,' Ed said. 'I don't want people making a fuss over me.'

Frank shook his son's hand. 'It's mighty grand to see you, son.' After a pause he added, 'Tom Pirelli told us you were dead.'

Ed smiled weakly. 'Don't blame him. I thought I was dead too.' His eyelids drooped and then flickered open again. 'Where is Tom? Did he deliver the watch?'

'Yes,' Mary answered quickly.

Ed let out a sigh. 'I knew I could rely on him.' Then he frowned and looked around the room. 'Where's Ethan?'

'I left him at home today, but I'll bring him tomorrow.'

'Good. I gotta see the General. How is he?'

'He's fine,' Mary assured him. 'He's longing to see you.'

His eyes drifted closed again and this time they stayed closed.

Alarmed, Mary looked to the nurse. 'Is he all right?'

'There's no change in his condition,' she said, 'but he needs to be left to rest now.'

By the time Mary arrived home from her long day at the hospital she was worn out and headachy. She needed a long soak in a hot bath and then perhaps she would dial out for a pizza. Ethan loved pizza and she was too tired to bother with cooking tonight.

The last thing she needed or expected, as she drove into her driveway, was to be greeted by the piercing sound of an electric drill. What the heck was going on? Tom had offered to babysit Ethan—a simple task involving peanut butter sandwiches, reading her son's favourite books and playing endless games of dominoes. Since when did an electric drill fit into *that* scene?

Puzzled, and faintly alarmed, she parked her car next to the snazzy black Jeep Tom had hired and hurried into the house via the back door. The whining racket came from upstairs and threatened to penetrate her skull. It was so loud that when she called out a greeting no one heard her. *Great!* Just what she needed. *Not!*

Peeved, she climbed the stairs and marched down the hallway, primed to demand a halt to such thoughtlessness. Midway down the hall she encountered pages from the *Washington Post* spread on the floor and, on top of them, a scattering of wood shavings, a tube of wood glue and an assortment of pliers and screwdrivers.

Then she saw Ethan, standing in the bathroom doorway.

'What's going on?' she demanded.

'Oh, hi, Mum. I'm helping Tom.' He held out something small, metallic and shiny. 'I'm passing up the screws to him.'

Tom poked his head around the doorway and his dark eyes flashed as he smiled at her. 'Hi,' he said.

Mary stepped closer and saw that he'd removed the bathroom door. Worse. He'd taken his shirt off. Her mouth went dry and, heaven help her, she couldn't help staring. Once upon a time she had been completely familiar with every inch of Tom's body. Now his shoulders were much broader than she remembered—and his arms were definitely more muscular, his stomach supertaut and tanned. Healthy.

And somehow his potent masculinity bothered her more than the mess and the noise. It was *too* much.

'What is it with Australian males?' she cried. 'Why do you all have to go around with your shirts off flexing your muscles?'

Tom frowned. 'I was just trying to keep my shirt clean.'

'Well, it's about time you remembered you're in America. They have dress standards in this country.' She stabbed the air with a belligerent finger, pointing at the door propped against the bathroom wall. 'And what on earth are you doing to my bathroom?'

'The door wouldn't close properly,' he said patiently. 'So Ethan and I thought we'd fix it.'

About to respond with another testy comment, she discovered that her urge to rant was diminishing. It was getting harder to stay annoyed. Tom was doing her a favour. Ethan had known for some time that she hated the way the bathroom latch didn't work.

'I was hoping to be done before you got back,' Tom said.

Mary sighed. 'Ed needed to sleep again, so I came home early.'

The amused light in his eyes faded. 'How is Ed? Do you have any more news?'

'No, not since I rang you at lunchtime. They're still very worried about his kidneys. There seems to be lasting damage from the jungle virus.'

'Will he need dialysis?'

'Perhaps.' She sighed again, and tried to signal with her eyes that she didn't want to say more in front of Ethan.

'Hang in there, Mary,' Tom said gently. 'Ed's damn tough.'

'Yes.' She managed a tired smile and drew in a deep breath as she surveyed his handiwork.

Tom turned back to the door.

And Mary saw the scar.

It was like a jagged white new moon, carved deeply into his back, just above his shoulderblade. The skin around it was puckered.

'What happened, Tom?' she cried, staring at it.

'I've repositioned the strike plate and now I just need to adjust the hinges.'

'No, I mean what happened to you? That scar.'

'Oh, that,' he said. 'Afghanistan, a couple of years ago.'

Suddenly she was stricken with guilt. She had no right to be taking such a keen interest in Tom Pirelli's body. And trying to argue with herself that it was OK to switch from admiring his muscles to concern over his scar was feeble.

Tom gestured to the newspapers on the floor. 'Sorry about the mess, but this isn't a big job. I should be finished soon. A couple of the screws were stripped bare, so we got new ones.' To Ethan he said, 'Can you pass me another screw, mate?'

'Sure, boss.' Ethan flashed Mary a grin. 'I'm Tom's apprentice.'

Ethan's obvious happiness melted the last of her annoyance. 'So you've had an exciting day?' she asked, ruffling his hair.

The boy's eyes shone and he nodded.

Mary had to blink, and she quickly returned her attention to the assortment of gear scattered at her feet. 'Where did you find all these tools, Tom?'

'Some were in your garage, and Ethan and I took a trip to the hardware store for the others.'

'I must say you're the most resourceful babysitter I've had. I guess I'd better make myself useful too. I'll go and dial up a pizza. I'm too pooped to cook.'

'No need,' Tom said. 'Dinner's been taken care of.'

'What?'

He lifted a massive shoulder in a shrug. 'It's nothing flash, but I threw together a kind of bolognese pasta, so you can just heat it up when you're ready.'

Mary's jaw dropped as she sagged against the wall and gaped at him. 'Goodness, Tom, I'm—I'm—' She pressed her fingers against her throbbing temple. 'I don't know what to say—except—thank you.'

Tom looked embarrassed and turned his attention to screwing the hinge in place.

'I'll go check my e-mail, then,' she said. 'And, when you're finished, I'd love a long hot soak in that tub.'

'I'll have it ready in no time.'

Tom was as good as his word. By the time Mary emerged from the newly secured bathroom, freshly bathed and changed into comfortable trousers and T-shirt, the newspapers, wood-shavings and tools were cleared away, and she came into the kitchen to find it redolent with the welcoming aroma of tomatoes, basil and oregano. 'What smells so good?'

Tom turned, grinning. 'You. What did you put in that bath water?'

She smiled and rolled her eyes. 'Secret women's business.'

She told herself that only a wicked, wanton, *contrary* woman would be disappointed that he was wearing his shirt again. Approaching the stove, she asked, 'Is this one of your nonna's famous recipes?'

'A poor imitation of the real thing, I'm afraid.' He turned down the flame and set the wooden spoon aside. 'Shouldn't take too long to reheat.'

'It looks good and smells great. Thanks so much.'

From outside came the sound of a ball bouncing on concrete. 'Is Ethan playing out there?'

'Yes, he's full of beans today.'

'He's obviously enjoyed your company.' She paused. 'I'm dreading taking him to the hospital tomorrow. I don't know how to prepare him for the changes in Ed.'

At the mention of Ed the atmosphere in the room became tense again.

'Ethan and I had a little chat about visiting Ed today,' Tom said.

'What did you tell him?'

'Just that there will be a whole stack of equipment, kind of like the inside of a spaceship, and his dad will be very sleepy and doped up with medicine.'

'I hope it won't frighten him.'

A grimace tightened Tom's features momentarily. 'I guess you should keep the visit short.'

'Yes. And will you visit too? Ed's very keen to see you.'

'Yes, I'll go tomorrow if it's not too soon.'

Mary nodded. It felt so strange to be talking like this to Tom, as if their past had never happened, as if he was merely a friend of Ed's, whom she'd met a few days ago.

'I'm sure seeing you will do him the world of good,' she said.

'So if Ethan and I both visit Ed briefly in the morning—Ethan first, then me—I may as well take Ethan on to school afterwards, or bring him back here, or wherever you think is best.'

'But I can't keep imposing on you.'

Tom held up his hand like a cop halting traffic. 'Mary, Ed wasn't just any old buddy. We were really close mates. Let me do this for him. Besides, it makes sense if I'm going to be there anyway and it leaves you free to stay on with Ed.'

'It's a very kind offer, but—'

Suddenly the whole lie felt too big. How could she go on hiding the truth from Tom? Seeing him with Ethan made her too painfully aware of how much he'd been denied. The boy was *his son*. Flesh of his flesh. Together she and Tom had made Ethan. He was a living symbol of their passion.

She couldn't bear to imagine her own life without her little man. When she thought about the wonderful baby years Tom had missed she wanted to weep as if it were her own loss.

'Mary, stop hesitating. Just say yes. I won't be here for much longer, so make use of me while you can.'

When she didn't object he reached over and scooped up his car keys from the kitchen counter. 'So that's settled?'

'I seem to spend all my time saying thank you,' she said. 'But I am truly, truly grateful for your help.'

'OK, I'll head off now.'

'You're not staying to eat with us?'

'I'll eat back at the hotel.'

'But you've gone to so much trouble.' Mary peered into the pot and gave it a stir with the wooden spoon. 'And there's masses of food. You must stay and have some.'

She glanced back at him, offering him a shy smile of encouragement, but her smile died when she saw the way he was looking at her.

'I don't think it's a good idea,' he said, and the dark intensity in his eyes sent her pulse-rate galloping.

She looked away.

She understood exactly why he wanted to get away. They were both acutely aware that spending time alone together was dangerous.

They were remembering *yesterday's kiss*.

Yesterday, she and Tom had been given one cruelly brief window of opportunity to openly express their feelings for each other, and now, with Ed's return, that chance was closed to them again. *For ever.*

She saw the pain of that knowledge in Tom's eyes.

Threading nervous hands through her hair, she was compelled to ask, 'Do you feel as if fate is playing games with us, Tom?'

CHAPTER TEN

MARY'S heart pounded in her ears as she watched Tom consider her question.

Leaning one hip against a cupboard, he gave a little toss of his car keys from one hand to the other. 'I don't think we can lay the blame completely with fate. We haven't been helpless victims, without any choice.'

'Haven't we? Sometimes I feel as if I've lived my whole life in something like a—a pinball machine, getting whacked in one direction then another. I don't think I've had much choice.'

Tom pocketed the keys. 'If you're talking about what's happened to us, Mary, there have been choices every step of the way.'

'When?'

'You chose to believe your father. You chose to marry Ed.'

His words stung. 'In that case I suppose I could say that you chose to give up trying to find me.'

'Yes,' he admitted.

'Oh, heavens, I'm sorry, Tom. I shouldn't have started this silly conversation. If anyone's a victim, it's poor Ed.' Her face crumpled and she pressed a fisted hand against her trembling mouth.

Tom grimaced but he didn't move. He stood very still, watching her, his tension visible in the set of his shoulders and the muscles working in his jaw.

Mary stared back at him.

Outside in the backyard, Ethan's basketball continued to bounce on the concrete path.

Taking a deep breath, she looked away. 'I hope you don't mind my saying this, Tom, but—I—I wanted to let you know, that if I were still free—'

Tears threatened and she swiped blindly at her eyes with her sleeve. 'We had a choice yesterday, and I'm ashamed to admit this, I—I wish we'd made love.' Turning to him, her voice trembled as she asked, 'Am I being impossibly selfish to tell you this?'

'Oh, Mary.'

In a heartbeat Tom was beside her, dragging her into his arms, enfolding her. 'You don't have the monopoly on selfishness, sweetheart. All I think about is how much I want you. You have no idea. I crave you. I can't bear the thought of losing you again. But you know it would have been a mistake. Think how sick we'd have felt when we learned about Ed.'

'Yes.' A deep sigh seeped from her as she rested her forehead against his shoulder. 'The problem is I seem to be losing my grip on what's right and wrong. Nothing seems to make sense any more. I'd hate to have broken my wedding vows, I couldn't bear to hurt Ed, but at the same time my heart tells me that loving you could never be a mistake.'

Tom made a low, desperate sound as he hugged her tight. 'This whole thing is a mess, but the one good thing is that we have total honesty between the three of us— you, me and Ed. Whatever happens, that's got to stay important.'

Total honesty?

Mary's heart stood still. The blood in her veins turned to ice. Dear Lord, what would Tom think of her honesty if he knew about Ethan? She pulled out of his arms.

'Mary, what's the matter?'

She couldn't tell him. Not now. Tomorrow morning he and Ethan would both be seeing Ed. If the truth came out now it could spoil their reunion. And Ed needed Tom's wholehearted support. But after that she had to tell Tom. Tomorrow…

'Mary, don't look like that. Tell me what's upset you.'

Oh, dear, what could she say? 'Ed—Ed doesn't know about—about you and me—in the past. He knows there was someone else I'd planned to marry, but he doesn't know details. When you go to see him you must promise me that you won't tell him anything about—us.'

He released a quick sigh of relief. 'Yes, of course. I figured he couldn't have known.' He took a step back away from her. 'And now I'd better go.'

'Yes.'

He tried to smile. 'Don't let that pasta dry out.'

'No.'

'Goodbye, Mary.'

'I'll see you in the morning.'

Ethan and Mary weren't around when Tom arrived to see Ed. When he was shown into the hospital room he was not suddenly shocked to see how pale and wasted his mate was. He'd been preparing himself, imagining what Ed had been through. And he'd seen it too many times before—badly injured comrades with battle wounds, trying to make the best of it.

As he approached the bed Ed's eyes opened and his face lit up, breaking, for a moment, into a ghostly replica of the old Ed McBride thousand-kilowatt smile. 'Tom, old buddy, good to see you.'

'G'day mate.' Tom shook his hand. 'Looks like you did a number on yourself.'

'I reckon I must have.'

His fingers slipped from the hand clasp and Tom felt a stab of alarm as a look of desolate weariness settled over his friend's features.

Taking a seat, he waited quietly by the bed, thinking of the times he and Ed had pulled each other back from the brink of death. Was it possible again this time?

After a while Ed rallied again. 'Aren't you going to congratulate me, Tom? I finally did something even Captain Pirelli of the Australian SAS wouldn't attempt. I free fell one hundred feet into a tropical rainforest.'

'I know, mate. I was there, remember? I'm more than impressed. I'd really written you off, Ed. I was sure you'd bought it.'

'The thick canopy saved me. But us Yanks are hard to kill…if you haven't noticed.'

'Thank God the local militia found you and not the terrorists.'

'Yeah.' Ed smiled again. 'So… What do you think of my Mary?'

A rush of adrenalin engulfed Tom. He cleared his throat. 'She's…very lovely. You're a lucky man.'

'I sure am. It was thinking about Mary and Ethan that kept me going. By the way, thanks for bringing back the watch.'

Tom nodded.

'You've met Ethan, haven't you?'

'Yeah, mate. He's a chip off the old block, for sure—a great little bloke.'

Ed sighed and winced as he moved his head into a new position on the pillow. 'I should tell you. He's my boy, Tom, but…' His eyelids drooped.

'Don't tire yourself out, mate. You don't have to talk.'

'No, I want to tell you…'cause you went to so much

trouble to bring the watch and—and I'll feel better if I explain.'

Tom waited while Ed rested again. When his eyes opened he said, 'Ethan's not really a chip off *this* old block.'

'What do you mean?'

'I'm not his natural father.'

'What?'

'I had the mumps real bad when I was fourteen and I can't have kids. I'm firing blanks.'

A bomb detonated in the centre of Tom's chest.

'When I met Mary Ethan was about eighteen months old. He's actually a little Aussie, Tom. One of your lot.'

Tom's insides were exploding. No, he was *imploding*. He was caving inwards. Disintegrating.

Collapsing in on himself, piece by piece.

It couldn't be true. An Australian couldn't be Ethan's father. Ed was his father. Mary would have told him if it was someone else—if it was... Oh, no. No! *No!*

'How—how old is he?' he managed to ask, and he dreaded the answer. He'd never given any thought to Ethan's age. A little boy was just a little boy—like a puppy—age wasn't an important factor.

'He'll be seven next month—in August.'

Seven! Covering his face with his hands, Tom struggled to breathe. If the boy was turning seven, it meant...

Ethan had to be his son.

How could Mary have hidden the truth from him for all these years? How could she have done that?

'Hey, Tom, are you OK?'

Squeezing his eyes tightly shut, Tom struggled to control himself. One thing Ed didn't need was someone having a nervous breakdown at his bedside.

'Don't let it upset you,' Ed said. 'Mary got over the Aussie. We've been happy.'

'Yeah,' Tom said, breathing deeply. 'Of course you've been happy. Mary was damn lucky she found you, man. So was Ethan.'

Ed relaxed back onto his pillow, a faint smile playing on his lips. With a supreme effort of will Tom forced a lid on his raging feelings and focused on his friend. He couldn't give in to self-pity now. Ed had no idea of the havoc he'd just caused and the poor bloke was fighting for his life.

When Ed tried to talk again he had to pause to catch his breath. 'We both know…worse things to come for Mary…she'll need some support.'

'Don't start talking negative, mate,' Tom insisted gruffly. 'You're tougher than nails. You're the miracle man. You're going to pull through this.'

'I don't know, buddy.' Ed shook his head slowly and his eyes closed again. 'I only hung on this long by being stubborn, but I'm too damn tired…' He seemed to sink into his pillow.

Tears burned Tom's eyes and dammed his throat. Choking with emotion, he reached out and covered Ed's thin hand with his. 'You'll tell your grandkids about all this, buddy, and the story will get bigger and bigger each year. You'll add a few feet to the fall every time you tell it.'

Ed didn't reply.

'You'll be fine, mate.'

A nurse bustled into the room and leaned over the bed to check her patient. She frowned and quickly pressed a pager clipped to her belt.

'I'm afraid you must leave now, sir,' she said. 'The doctor is on his way.'

At the door Tom turned, overwhelmed by a torrent of conflicting emotions. For a fleeting moment he fancied there was something else Ed had wanted to tell him, but then the nurse leaned over the bed again and obscured his view and, moments later, a doctor came hurrying down the corridor.

'I don't want to go to school.'

Mary's heart sank when she saw the stubborn determination in her son's eyes. 'But you've missed two days already. Think of all the fun you're missing out on. Don't you want to see your friends?'

'No.' Ethan sat stiffly on the vinyl-covered armchair in the hospital foyer and glowered at Mary.

'But surely you want to play with Luke and Caleb?'

'Nope.'

'Oh, Ethan, you used to love school. Why don't you want to go?'

'I just don't. I don't like it any more. It's boring.'

'But won't it be fun to ride there in Tom's Jeep?'

For a moment the boy's eyes widened with sudden interest and Mary sensed success, but then he sighed and slumped lower in the chair. 'Nope.'

'Look, darling, I know you're upset about Daddy, but he wants you to go to school. You'll make him happy if you go.'

'How do you know?'

'He's told me lots of times. He's so proud of how clever you are.'

'I'm not clever.'

Mary frowned. This was a new reaction she hadn't encountered before. 'What makes you think you're not clever?'

Ethan shrugged and his lower lip pushed forward. He refused to look her in the eye.

'Has something happened at school to upset you?'

He made a point of avoiding her gaze, swinging around in his chair and looking back across the reception area to the start of the corridor that led to Ed's ward. But his manner changed when he pointed suddenly. 'Look, there's Tom.'

Mary turned, caught sight of Tom, and felt her spirits lift, almost as if she'd been kicked high in the air like a football, but the sensation quickly collapsed when she saw the dark look on his face.

Heaven have mercy, what's happened? Leaping to her feet, she hurried across the foyer. 'What is it, Tom? Is it Ed?'

He stared at her with a kind of dazed horror.

'Tom, tell me what's the matter. How's Ed?'

'I'm not sure,' he said at last, as if her question had taken ages to register. 'The nurse called for the doctor, and they asked me to leave.'

'Oh, heavens. I'll go straight down there and see what's happened. How did Ed seem to you?'

'Very sleepy.' Tom turned his attention to Ethan, standing beside her.

'I've been telling Ethan that you've offered to drive him to school in your Jeep.'

He nodded, but his dazed expression had been replaced by a look of cool disdain and Mary felt compelled to ask, 'Is that still OK with you?'

His eyes met hers, piercing her with an expression that couldn't have been any harder or more contemptuous if she'd been an enemy in his sights. 'I'll take him,' he said. 'But at some stage today I need to have a talk with you. About Ethan's birthday.'

His *birthday*? Mary choked and her legs almost collapsed beneath her. What had the men talked about?
What had happened? Had the truth come out?

Rendered speechless, she stared back at Tom. She
wasn't sure she could deal with another problem right
now. Ed was facing a crisis, Ethan seemed to be dealing
with some kind of dilemma about school and now *this*...

From somewhere nearby she heard Ethan's piping
voice. 'I don't want to go to school.' Then his voice
seemed to come from further away. 'You can't make me
go to school. I'm not going.'

And suddenly Tom was jumping past her, shouting,
'Ethan!'

She turned to see her son running towards the hospital
entrance and Tom dashing after him.

She tried to run after them, but her legs were shaking
so badly she had to give up and lean against the reception desk, watching as Tom reached her boy and grabbed
his hand before he got outside. *Thank heavens.*

Bracing herself against the desk, she saw her son's
stormy face as Tom crouched beside him. Tom placed
a firm hand on each of Ethan's shoulders and turned the
boy till he stood square in front of him, eye to eye, and
then Tom spoke to the boy quietly. She could see that
Ethan was listening and calming down.

Quite quickly they seemed to reach some kind of
agreement. Tom rose, took Ethan's hand, and the two of
them began to walk back to her. Mary watched with her
own hands pressed against her quaking heart.

'Ethan's coming with me,' Tom told her quietly.

She gulped. Was she imagining the possessive tone in
his voice? 'Are you taking him to school?'

'We're going to have a chat about school,' Tom said.
'Maybe we'll be able to sort a few things out.'

There was a new air of cool authority about Tom. What had caused it? Was this the other side of Tom she'd never seen—Captain Pirelli, the Special Operative? What few things did he want to sort out?

It was so hard to ask questions with Ethan listening—impossible to ask what Tom had meant when he spoke of Ethan's birthday. She had no choice but to trust him.

And a well-remembered voice inside her whispered: *You should always trust Tom. He's a Very Nice-a Boy.*

'I've rung Mrs Spencer and explained that Ethan will be coming later today,' she said.

Ethan frowned when she said that, but then he looked up at Tom and the frown became more hopeful.

Mary drew a sharp breath. 'Thanks, Tom, I'll contact you on your cellphone around lunchtime.'

'Yeah, you do that.' His tone suggested that they had a great deal to discuss.

'And now I'd better hurry along to see Ed.'

'I hope he's OK. They probably just needed to stabilise him.'

'Yes.' She knelt quickly to press a kiss on Ethan's cheek. 'Promise me you won't try to run away again.'

'No, Mummy.'

'Be good for Tom.'

There was so much more she needed to say—to Tom, to Ethan—but right now it was Ed who needed her most of all.

With a final quick hug for Ethan, she stood. 'Thanks again, Tom.'

Then she turned and hurried away from them.

Tom marvelled that he was keeping his cool.

Of course it was all a façade. He was acting cool on the outside. Low voice. Measured walking pace. Calm, collected body language. But his coolness was only skin-deep. Inside, he was stirred to the max.

This small boy walking beside him and holding his hand was his son.

His and Mary's. They'd made him together. Hell, he even knew *when* they'd made Ethan. It must have happened that time they went to the island and had to stay overnight unexpectedly because of a storm. They'd been so swept away by the wild night and their even wilder passion that they hadn't given a thought to consequences.

And here were the consequences...this pint-sized package. This miniature man with soft blond hair and big brown eyes...who didn't want to go to school.

Welcome to fatherhood, Tom Pirelli.

To add insult to injury, he didn't have the option of confronting Mary and demanding to know why she'd chosen not to tell him about his son. Ed's needs were dire and required immediate attention; Tom's would have to wait. And, in the meantime, he had to deal with Ethan.

With Ethan's hand in his, they walked through the hospital grounds till they found shaded parkland.

'This look OK to you?' Tom asked.

Ethan nodded.

'You want to sit on a park bench or stretch out on the grass?'

'The grass.'

'OK.' Lowering himself to the ground, Tom rested his back against a solid maple trunk and stretched his long legs in front of him. Ethan sat hunched over, with his arms wrapped around his skinny knees as he stared at the ground.

'So, do you want to tell me about school?'

The boy didn't answer.

Leaning sideways, Tom plucked one of the longer blades of grass that grew close to the trunk. He chewed its juicy stem. 'You like to eat grass?'

Ethan's eyes grew round with surprise, but he nodded.

Tom plucked another stem and handed it to him. 'Here, try this.'

Ethan nibbled the grass, and a reluctant smile brought dimples to his cheeks and a sparkle to his eyes. He was a damn cute kid. Until now Tom had only noticed the boy's likeness to Mary, but now he found himself hunting for visible links between himself and the boy, and he decided that there was a disquieting familiarity about Ethan's eyes.

After a stretch of silence Tom said, 'So what's your teacher's name?'

'Mrs Spencer.'

'What's she like?'

Ethan shrugged.

'Is she stroppy?'

'What's stroppy?'

'Crabby. Angry. Sorry, I guess it's an Australian word.'

'Oh.'

'So does Mrs Spencer get upset?'

'Yeah, she yells sometimes.'

'Teachers who yell are the pits. Does she shout at all the kids?' he asked, keeping his voice excessively casual.

'Yes.'

'That's tough.'

A blue jay swooped out of a tree and pecked at an insect in the grass and they both watched it.

'So...what do you reckon makes Mrs Spencer get so mad?'

Ethan turned and looked at Tom. 'She doesn't like the way I draw.'

'No kidding? But your drawings are terrific. I saw your work stuck up on the fridge.'

'But I use the wrong hand to hold the pencil.'

'What hand do you draw with?'

Solemnly Ethan held up both hands. And a cold sweat crept up Tom's back. Goosebumps broke out on his arms and he seemed to lose his ability to breathe. Eventually he said, 'Are you telling me you can draw with either hand?'

'Yeah.' Ethan smiled, apparently pleased that Tom understood. 'Some days I draw or write with this hand, and some days I use this hand, and Mrs Spencer gets cross. She wants me to write and draw everything with my right hand all the time, but I keep forgetting.'

Struggling to clear the lump of emotion in his throat, Tom said, 'That's because you're ambidextrous.'

'Am I?' Ethan digested this news and then asked, 'Is that bad?'

'No way, mate. Watch this.' Pulling a small spiral notebook and pen from his pocket, Tom drew a swift sketch of a squirrel. Then he switched hands and drew another.

'Wow!' exclaimed Ethan excitedly. 'You do it with both hands too. You're the same as me.'

'Yeah.'

'How come?' the boy asked, frowning.

'It's just—ah—the way we're made. But it's not a problem. You'll find it comes in handy when you're older. You'll be able to catch and throw balls and shoot goals with both hands.'

'I won't get into trouble?'

Tom smiled. 'Not a chance, mate. If you can slam-dunk with your left or your right hand you'll be a champion.'

Ethan picked up the notebook and studied the two drawings with wide-eyed wonder.

'You know, kid,' Tom said, 'what you need for Mrs Spencer's class is a watch.'

'Like the one you brought home from my dad?'

'Well, that one's a bit fancy for school. But we could call in at a store on our way across town and see if we can find one that's just right. The secret is to strap the watch to your right wrist, so when you get to school you can always remember to pick up your pencil with that hand.'

Staring at his right wrist, Ethan nodded. 'A watch would be neat. Wow, thanks Tom. Is that what you wanted to tell Mum about my birthday? Is the watch my early birthday present?'

'Yeah.' Tom grimaced. 'Something like that.'

By lunchtime Ed's crisis was over. His condition had improved marginally, but he was still sleepy, so Mary left him to nap while she went to the hospital canteen and bought a sandwich and a cup of coffee, then carried them outside, looking for somewhere quiet and restful to eat.

She found a free bench in the shade of an enormous old oak tree, with a view of rose gardens at their summer best. But after two bites of her sandwich she set the food aside; she was too anxious to eat.

There seemed to be no respite from worry—Ed's alarming condition, Ethan's refusal to go to school and now Tom's barely controlled anger. He wanted to discuss Ethan's *birthday*.

It was the way he'd said the word 'birthday', weighting it with threatening significance, that bothered her. It had to mean...

She dragged in a nervous breath. With Ed so ill she hadn't been able to ask him about his discussion with Tom, but whether Tom had found out the truth or not she *had* to talk to him about it. Now. The time had come. She should phone him before she lost the nerve.

Her hands shook as she keyed his number into her cellphone.

He answered almost immediately. 'Pirelli.'

'Tom, it's Mary.'

'Yeah, stay there. I'm coming right over.'

'Coming?' Alarmed, she scanned the stretch of gardens in front of her. 'Where—where are you?'

'About fifty metres behind you.'

She spun around wildly and saw Tom striding across the park towards her, his long legs eating up the short distance that separated them.

'I wanted to talk to you face to face,' he said into the phone.

Disconnecting, she dropped the phone into her handbag as if it had burned her. As he drew closer she saw the dark coldness shadowing his face and her heart began to thump. Her terrible morning was about to take one more turn for the worse.

He came to a halt in front of her. 'How's Ed?' he asked.

'He's stabilised.' She jumped to her feet. Tom was far too tall and intimidating for her to remain seated. 'But I'm afraid the doctors aren't looking too happy. I get the feeling they'd expected faster improvement.'

'Medicos are often impatient.'

'I guess so.' She looked at him anxiously. 'How has your morning been, Tom? I've been keeping my fingers crossed that Ethan would behave for you.'

Without smiling, he said, 'Perhaps the crossed fingers did the trick. Ethan's been good as gold.'

'Did he go to school?'

'Rushed off like a fruit bat heading for a mango tree.'

'That's fantastic.' She tried to sound pleased, but any sense of relief she might have felt was kept at bay by the hardness in Tom's face and the tension that burned inside her. How was she going to work up the courage to tell him what she must? 'You seem to be able to work miracles with Ethan.'

He didn't respond.

Mary gulped. This was *The Moment*. She chewed her lip nervously. 'Would you like to sit down?'

'Sure.'

They sat, carefully apart—Mary very upright and with her knees primly together—Tom more casual, with one knee bent and the other stretched comfortably in front of him.

Hooking an elbow over the back of the wooden seat, he slowly turned towards her. 'Do you know why your son has been avoiding school?'

He sounded so annoyingly like a prosecuting attorney in a courtroom drama that Mary was instantly on the defence. 'Ethan's been very upset about Ed, of course.'

'Yes, Mary, but surely you've noticed there's something else that's been bothering him?'

What was this? Twenty questions: category—motherhood?

'I had begun to wonder if there's something happening at school to upset him. This morning he seemed bothered about not being clever.'

Tom nodded. 'His teacher has been hassling him about his writing.'

'But there's nothing wrong with his writing.'

'Mrs Spencer is insisting that he has to use his right hand.' After a carefully timed pause, Tom added, '*Only* his right hand.'

'He—he didn't tell me that.'

Tom was watching her with the fierce intensity of a falcon swooping towards its prey. 'That kind of restriction causes a small dilemma for Ethan, doesn't it?'

'Do-does it?'

'I'm sure you must be aware that your son is ambidextrous.'

'I was beginning to wonder. I wasn't sure. I—'

Tom continued. 'Excuse the pun, but it's kind of *handy* that I happen to be ambidextrous too.'

She didn't answer—*couldn't* answer because her mouth was too dry and her heart too frantic. She stared at the grass at her feet and tried to say yes, but nothing emerged except a tiny squeak. Tom knew about Ethan, but he was dragging this conversation out—making her suffer.

'I was able to give Ethan a couple of hints on how to keep the teacher happy,' he said, his voice losing warmth with every syllable.

Mary slumped on the park bench. 'I know where this conversation is heading, Tom. I'm sorry you found out this way. I was planning to talk to you about—about Ethan.'

'When?'

'Today. This afternoon. Now.'

He released a cold chuckle. 'Nice timing, Mary, but

your husband beat you to it. Not that the poor guy knew the significance of what he told me.'

'Tom, please try to understand.'

'Oh I understand. What I understand most is that your news is almost eight years too late.'

A cry of helpless, desperate anger broke from her. It was so easy for Tom to sit there in cold-hearted judgement. He had no idea what it had been like for her, when she was alone and pregnant, cut off from every support except her hostile parents.

'I couldn't tell you eight years ago. You know what happened. I explained how I thought you wanted to get away from me to Perth.'

He shook his head. 'The thing I don't understand is why you believed any of that bull your father fed you. And I don't understand how you could give birth to my son and not make any attempt to contact me. I especially don't understand how you were so happy to let another man become his father.'

Pain dammed Mary's throat. Tears slid down her cheeks. 'By the time I found out I was pregnant you were gone. Out of my life.'

She looked at Tom again and then wished she hadn't. He showed no sign that he understood her despair. If anything, his expression was angrier than it had been before.

'What about *now*?' he demanded. 'I've been here since last Friday. That's five days, Mary. On Sunday you went through a very nice performance of claiming to love me—'

'Don't, Tom. Please don't suggest that was pretence.'

For a moment some of the hardness left his face. A fleeting, lost expression dimmed the anger in his eyes and Mary saw the way his throat worked.

'You still forgot to mention our son,' he said, his voice as choked as hers. 'And now you expect me to say, That's fine, Mary, I understand perfectly.'

'Tom, I'm sorry. I'm so sorry.'

He rose quickly, as if he needed to distance himself from her tears. 'I'm beyond sorry.' He glanced at his watch and grimaced. 'This is a hell of a way to part, but I'm heading off now. There's no place for me here.'

She leapt to her feet again. 'Don't go now. Please don't rush off so quickly. I can't bear to see you so angry.'

'You can't bear it, Mary? Do you think I'm enjoying this? I've been a lone wolf in the Army all these years and now, at last, I'm going home to my family, and I've just discovered that I'm leaving a little Pirelli descendant behind me, over here.'

'Then stay, Tom,' she pleaded, clutching desperately at straws. 'Give us time to sort this out.'

'What's the point in staying? What is there to sort out?'

'But if you leave now you'll be walking away from Ethan too.'

'You, Ed and Ethan are a family. If I try to enter the loop I'll just make things worse. Ed's got more than enough to deal with. And Ethan can't be told. It would stuff *him* up completely. As for you—I—I certainly need to stay well away from you.'

He gave an impatient shake of his head. 'I've thought about this all morning, and the best possible thing I can do for everyone is to get the hell back to the other side of the world and let you and Ed and Ethan get on with your lives.'

In her head his words made perfect sense, but in her

heart they made no sense at all. 'Won't you at least see Ed again before you go?'

'No, Mary, he's got all the support he needs—the best medical care in the world, a loving family. The way I feel now, I'd only get in the way.'

She didn't care that tears were running uncontrollably down her cheeks. It was awful to be saying goodbye to Tom, but so much worse to see the lack of sympathy in his eyes—to be parting in anger and misunderstanding.

Again.

'I just wish I'd handed over the bloody watch and cleared off last Friday morning,' he said.

And then he kept walking.

CHAPTER ELEVEN

'Now, remember, don't be too boisterous,' Mary warned Ethan as they neared Ed's hospital room. 'No more climbing up on to Daddy's bed. You don't want to make him seasick.'

'How can he be seasick when he's in a bed?'

Mary rolled her eyes. 'Just do as I ask, please. Stay off the bed until Daddy's ready to give you a hug and then I'll lift you.'

'OK.'

As they entered the room she was relieved to see that Ed was awake and looking quite bright. Each day he'd been looking a little stronger, and today his blue eyes lit up when he saw them.

'I drew a picture of you, Dad.' Ethan dragged a folded sheet of paper from his school bag and held it up proudly.

'Hey, that's terrific,' Ed said, grinning. 'That's a cool helicopter.'

'And that's you inside it.'

'OK, so who's the dude hanging on the rope?'

'Tom. This is a picture of you going on another mission with him. But you don't have to go down ropes any more.'

'Glad to hear it,' Ed said, and he winked at Mary. Then he asked Ethan, 'So how was school?'

'Terrific. Mrs Spencer's not stroppy with me any more.'

'Stroppy? What's that?'

'It's an Australian word. Tom taught it to me. It means cranky.'

'So you and Tom got along fine?' Ed said, reaching out to clasp Ethan's shoulder.

'Yep, and I never forget to use my right hand now.'

Ed frowned and his eyes questioned Mary.

'Ethan was writing with both hands,' she explained. 'His teacher didn't like it.'

Ed's eyebrows rose. 'The boy's ambidextrous?'

His question and the puzzled expression in his eyes sent Mary's heart racing. She hesitated before she answered, and Ethan beat her to it.

'That's right,' he said. 'That's the word. Tom told me he's ambi—'

'Ethan,' Mary cut in, her voice unnecessarily sharp.

Her son frowned and Ed looked at her strangely, as if she'd grown two heads, and she felt so upset she couldn't find the words to justify her interruption.

'Tom's like that too,' Ethan said. 'He can draw with both hands.'

'I know,' said Ed slowly. 'It's one of the things that makes him such a damn good soldier.'

His words were addressed to Ethan, but he was looking at Mary—looking at her with wide, questioning eyes. 'Mary,' he said, 'how about you give Ethan some money to go get a soda from the machine down the corridor?'

'Yes, s-sure.' Flustered, she fished around in her bag for suitable coins. Ed wanted to speak to her alone. About Tom. Her cheeks flamed as she pressed the money into Ethan's hand.

'Cool,' the boy said, smiling widely, surprised to be allowed this treat.

As he hurried off Mary was aware that Ed's eyes

hadn't left her and that her flushed face was a dead giveaway.

'This similarity between Tom and Ethan—it's not just a coincidence, is it?' Ed asked.

She closed her eyes, unable to bear the raw vulnerability in her husband's face. Tears welled behind her eyelids.

'Mary, sit down,' Ed said softly.

Fighting tears, she groped for the chair beside his bed.

'It's OK,' she heard him say.

'Oh, Ed.' The blur of her tears made his face waver before her. She reached a shaking hand to link with his and she felt his fingers grip her tightly.

'Does Tom know?' Ed asked.

'He didn't—until—until a few days ago.'

Drawing in a deep breath, Ed turned his gaze to the ceiling, then he let it out slowly. 'How did he take the news?'

Mary struggled to keep the threat of tears from her voice. 'It's all such a mess. He's gone back home to get out of our lives. He doesn't want to complicate things.'

'That sounds like the Tom I know.' Ed's eyes sought hers once more. 'But I'm still confused. I thought Ethan's father left you in the lurch.'

'No, Tom never knew.' Almost in a whisper, she added, 'My father made sure of that.'

Ed sighed and, to Mary's alarm, his Adam's apple slid up and down as if he were fighting to keep his emotions in check. Filled with remorse, she scooped up his hand and pressed her lips to it.

'Poor Mary,' he said. 'This past week must have been hell for you. You've had so much to deal with. You never fail to amaze me.'

'You're the amazing one, Ed, and it's how you feel that's important. You've been so ill—and now this.'

'I'm fine.' He cracked a small smile. 'Just think about it… You chose Tom and then me. You've got great taste, girl.'

Her heart full, she stroked his hand with her thumb.

'Now I know why Ethan's such a great little guy,' said Ed. 'I couldn't think of a better man than Tom to be his father.'

'You're Ethan's father, Ed. He adores you. You're the very best father a boy could have.'

'But at some stage Ethan will have to know.'

'Let's not worry about that now.'

They fell silent as they both thought about the future. After a bit Ed said, 'When Tom came to see me I virtually told him that I expected him to look after you and Ethan if something happened to me. I'm even happier about that now.'

Leaning close, Mary kissed his cheek. 'But you're going to be OK. You're getting better.'

He looked at her without smiling. 'Yeah, that's what everyone keeps telling me.'

It was humid inside Gina Pirelli's greenhouse, and by the time she'd finished watering her hanging baskets of ferns and begonias she was pleased to step outside on to the open lawn, where a fresh breeze came streaming up the side of the mountain.

As she stowed the hose away she smiled at the sight of her grandson standing at the edge of the terrace, hands on hips, staring off down the green valley to the hazy blue rainforest-clad mountains in the distance.

It was so good to have Tom home again. So good to know that at last she and his mother could stop worrying about their dear boy being blown to pieces by terrorists, or meeting with some other kind of dreadful accident like the one that had almost killed his American friend.

But there was something troubling him.

Tom was safe, but he wasn't happy. Gina had known that almost as soon as he'd walked through the kitchen door. Oh, he was pleased to be home. He'd been quite jubilant as he'd greeted her and his parents, his brother and sister-in-law and their children. There'd been bear hugs and kisses, laughter and back-slapping and a celebration dinner with his favourite gnocchi gorgonzola taking pride of place in the centre of the table.

But deep in Tom's soul there was dark unhappiness. Gina had sensed it last week and she was sure of it now. And she was quite certain she knew the source of his problem. The poor, darling boy was eating his heart out again over that Mary woman.

He hadn't mentioned her once since he'd come home, and that had to be a bad sign.

Right now, Tom seemed more upset than ever and, as she watched him, Gina's eyes widened with alarm. She thought she saw his shoulders shaking. *Caro Dio*, was he actually crying? She'd hadn't seen her fearless grandson cry since he was a bambino.

Shuffling close enough to make herself heard, she spoke softly. 'Toto.'

He spun around and her stomach dropped when she saw that his eyes were red from tears.

'Oh, it's you, Nonna,' he said. 'Hi.'

'What is it, *caro*? What's the matter?'

He held out an arm to her, as if inviting her close, and when she stepped nearer he wrapped his arm around her shoulders and she slipped hers around his waist, hugging him tight. Tom was so much bigger that her head rested well below his shoulder.

'I've just had bad news from the Australian Defence Headquarters in Canberra,' he told her. A grimace twisted his mouth. 'My friend Ed passed away.'

'Oh, dear, no. I thought you said he was getting better.'

'He was. Everything looked very hopeful for a while there. They said his fractures were healing well and they'd started him on dialysis and were hoping for a transplant down the track.' He drew in a shuddering breath. 'But apparently his system began to break down quite suddenly. Then his heart...'

'I'm so sorry.'

'Yeah.' Tom looked out across the valley. 'I've been worried about him. When I saw him in hospital he was being brave, but there was something in his eyes, as if he was distancing himself somehow. I think he knew.'

'Poor man,' Gina whispered.

'I was his captain on our last operation and the brass in Canberra want to fly me back for his funeral at Arlington Cemetery.'

'You'll go?'

'Yes, I must,' he said. 'But I'm not keen to go back so soon.' He released a long, drawn out sigh.

Gina's heart sank as she looked up at him. Tom's reaction was puzzling. He had lost soldier mates before this, and he'd often attended their funerals and had mourned for them by retreating into grim silence, but this time she was sure that there was something else troubling her grandson—something besides his friend's death. Was his Mary involved?

Arms linked, they stood without speaking and watched the breeze break up a bank of low cloud and send soft white trails of mist drifting down the hillside. Eventually, Gina could bear the silence no longer. 'You were so happy when you telephoned from Washington,' she said. 'Did something go wrong, *caro*?'

Sighing again, he said, 'It was already wrong, Nonna, but I was too flaming stupid to see it.'

'I've been worried about you ever since you came home.'

He gave her another one-armed hug. 'You worry too much, old girl. It's not good for your health.'

'This something that went wrong—it's Mary, isn't it?'

'Yes,' he admitted with obvious reluctance.

'You don't want to tell me about her?'

'I'd rather not. Not just now.'

After another stretch of silence she asked, 'Will you let me give you some advice, then?'

He smiled wryly. 'All my life you've been giving me advice. I wouldn't dare try to stop you now.'

'You might not like it.'

'I usually don't.'

'Your mother might never forgive me for this, but when you go back to America for this funeral I don't think you should come home again until you've got something settled with your Mary.'

He frowned. 'Don't you like having me home?'

'Of course I do, but I don't like to see you so unhappy. If you've left your heart behind in America, you're no good to us here.'

'But I'm not sure it's possible to settle this situation. It's complicated. I don't even know if I want to sort it out any more.'

Gina fixed him with her sternest glare. 'Believe me, you've got to sort it out before you come home again.'

As she watched Tom's thoughtful nod, Gina knew he

would do his utmost to follow her instruction and she prayed to God that she had given him the right advice.

Tom knew he could handle the funeral.

The dignified military rituals at Arlington National Cemetery involved a colour guard, a bugler and a firing party, as well as a casket team and a burial flag, and the combined effect created a very fitting tribute and a fine send-off for Ed. It was the events that would follow the funeral that Tom was dreading.

Going back to Mary's house. Going into her home, knowing that the old Tom, the naive, youthful Tom, would have wanted to defy convention, to sweep Mary and Ethan into his arms and carry them home with him. Knowing it just wasn't going to happen. Life wasn't that simple.

He wasn't that simple any more. And neither was Mary.

But, as it turned out, he couldn't go to her house straight from the service after all. He was detained at Arlington. An Australian Army liaison officer, a US Army Ranger colonel and some Pentagon staff all wanted to speak to him, and by the time they'd finished, Mary's house was filled to overflowing and he was able to slip inside unnoticed.

Mary, in her widow's black dress and with her hair drawn severely back from her face, was talking to a steady stream of people offering their condolences. From a discreet distance, Tom watched as she patiently greeted and spoke to them, and he noted the subtle changes wrought in her by the past harrowing weeks. She seemed more dignified, and yet softer, sadder.

Someone tapped his elbow and he turned to be greeted by a woman who introduced herself as one of Mary's friends. She pressed him to take a cup of coffee and a slice of chocolate cake and he retreated with these to a corner of the family room.

Susan McBride found him next.

'I'm so sorry that Ed didn't pull through,' he said after they'd exchanged greetings. 'If anyone deserved to make it, he did.'

'At least he came home to us for a little while,' Susan said, smiling bravely. Then she added more brightly, 'I'm glad I've found you, Tom. I've been wanting to thank you for your lovely letters and the flowers. They mean a lot to Frank and me. In fact I want to thank you for *everything*.'

He accepted her gratitude with a slight bow of his head, but he felt puzzled and not at all sure that he'd done much to deserve Susan's thanks.

'You've got your hands full there,' he said, acknowledging the tiny baby in her arms.

'Yes, this is David, our new little grandson.'

'Of course—your daughter's baby.'

'He doesn't look anything like our side of the family, though. He looks exactly like his father.'

Tom took this as a hint that he was expected to make a closer inspection of the tiny infant. But women's ability to find family likenesses in tiny, button-like features was a mystery to him. This kid had a monkey face with a minute red mouth and unfocused dark blue eyes—and, as far as Tom could tell, he looked remarkably like any other new baby.

'Well,' he said, 'he looks very healthy.' And then he couldn't help adding, 'I saw Ethan at the ceremony. Is he here now?'

'No. One of Mary's girlfriends has taken him over to her house to play with her children.'

'Good idea. I'm glad he doesn't have to try to cope with all this.'

'That's what we thought. Now, Tom, why don't we go and sit over there?' Susan said, nodding to a sofa. 'There's a coffee table, so you can put your cup and saucer down.'

Glad to be free of the dainty china, Tom agreed. They sat, and his attention was caught by a very large photo album left open to display pictures of Ed.

'You might like to have a look through that album,' Susan suggested. 'It's full of lovely family photos.'

He nodded without enthusiasm but made no move. The last thing he wanted was to sift through a series of happy snaps of Mary and Ed's marriage.

'Take a look at the photos at the very front,' Susan insisted, and when he hesitated she settled the baby on one arm, leaned forward and flipped the book back to the start.

Tom found himself faced with a set of photos of another newborn baby. Another monkey face with a tiny red mouth and unfocused dark blue eyes.

'That's Ethan,' she said.

Whack! In a split second the photos of the everyday, average baby took on new levels of significance. Tom darted a quick sideways glance to Susan and saw an unexpected camaraderie in her gaze. *She knew.*

'Do you…? Has Mary told you about—Ethan?'

'That he's your son?'

He nodded.

'She has, but she didn't have to tell me. I knew the moment I met you, Tom. It's the eyes. Look at them.'

Tom looked again, and felt his throat constrict. Armed with the knowledge that this was his son, he studied the tiny face more carefully and realised that it was possible to see a glimmer of the seven-year-old Ethan. He couldn't pinpoint *how* the baby resembled the boy, but the expression in the eyes was part of it. And, yes, perhaps he could see something of himself, too.

Susan said, 'By the time I met Ethan, when he was eighteen months old, his eyes were so dark they were almost black, just like yours.'

'He—he was kind of cute, wasn't he?'

'He was exceptionally cute.'

She turned more pages so that Tom could witness Ethan's progression of cuteness, from cute newborn to cute six-month-old, crawling on all fours, to cute toddler taking his first steps at around his first birthday.

There was a large photo of a snowy-headed Ethan stumbling on chubby legs towards Mary. She was kneeling on the grass with her arms outstretched, her lovely face alight with the bright glow of motherly pride.

Tom blinked and something the size of a houseboat lodged in his throat. 'It's very kind of you to show me these.'

'You're the boy's father. You deserve to see them, Tom.' Her eyes shone with sympathy. 'Mary told me why you left so suddenly after you found out about Ethan—how you decided that it would be in everyone's interests if you bowed out of the scene without making any demands.'

Tom stared at his clasped hands.

'You must have been shocked and hurt to find out that you had a son, but you put other people's needs before your own. I think that was very chivalrous of you.'

His throat was too damn choked for him to speak so he nodded his thanks.

Susan placed a comforting hand on his. 'You have no idea what a wonderful gift your son has been. Ed and

Mary couldn't have a baby of their own, but Ed was fiercely devoted to Ethan and incredibly proud of him. As far as our family is concerned, Ethan has been a very special bonus.'

Willing his emotions to settle, he dragged in a deep breath. 'It's always helpful to be shown a situation from another point of view. So thank you.'

'Thank *you*, Tom,' she said, giving his hand another reassuring squeeze. 'We've lost our son, but the little boy Ed loved will always be part of our extended family, no matter what the future may hold for Mary and Ethan.' She paused, letting the significance of her words take hold.

Tom wondered if she expected a comment from him, but he was still too overcome to speak.

She turned more pages in the book. 'Now, let me show you a photo of Ethan on his fifth birthday. Mary and Ed brought him down to our house…'

Mary was exhausted. The past weeks had been a dreadful blur of tortured, sleepless nights and anxious days. She'd been so worried about Ed and she'd tried hard to keep thoughts of Tom at a safe distance. But she'd lived on a knife-edge, while hope, fear, guilt and forbidden longing waged war inside her.

Now, as her guests were leaving, she scanned the room, hoping to find Tom. She'd seen him at the cemetery, looking unbearably handsome in his dark army green Australian ceremonial uniform and the sand-coloured beret of the SAS. He'd spoken to her briefly after the funeral, but she hadn't seen him since. She hadn't seen him come back to the house. Surely he wouldn't vanish again without some sort of contact?

Leaving the few remaining guests chatting in the

lounge with Frank McBride and Ed's sister, she walked down the hallway to the family room—and came to an amazed halt in the doorway when she saw Tom and Susan on the sofa, their heads together, smiling and pointing at photos. Susan seemed to be explaining something.

Even from this distance Mary knew they were looking at photos of Ethan. Her pulse went haywire. What was her mother-in-law telling Tom?

Susan looked up and saw her standing there. And then Tom looked up too, and the instant their eyes met a starburst exploded deep inside Mary. Oh, dear Lord, it was unforgivable to feel such a frenzied response to another man—today of all days—even if that man had been her first love—and the grand passion in her life.

'My goodness, Davy boy,' Susan said, suddenly levering herself forward on the sofa. 'We'd better go and find your mother. I'm sure you must be getting hungry again, you poor little munchkin.'

She was on her feet and had hurried out of the room before Mary could think of a valid reason to detain her. And suddenly she was alone in the room with Tom.

Her heartbeats ran wild as she walked towards him and, although she'd been talking to friends and acquaintances all morning, now she was with the one person she wanted to speak to and she didn't know what to say. He'd been so angry when he'd left and she'd had no communication with him since. Was he still angry?

As she reached him he set the album back on the coffee table and rose to his feet. His face gave nothing away. 'Hello, Mary.'

'Hello, Tom.' She took a deep breath. 'It was very good of you to come all the way back from Australia for the funeral.'

'I'm glad I came,' he said. 'It was a very moving service.'

She nodded. 'I know it sounds a bit weird, but I think Ed would have liked it.'

'I'm sure he would have.'

An awkward silence fell over them.

'I saw you talking to Colonel Maguire and some of the fellows from the Pentagon and I thought they might have whisked you off with them,' she said.

'They chewed my ear for quite a while, but then I got away. You've had a busy morning.'

'Yes.' Looking down at the album, she said nervously, 'You've found the photos.'

'Yes, I'm now fully informed about Ethan's days as an ankle-biter.'

'What—what do you think of them?'

'I can see that he's been a terrific little bloke right from the start,' he said without smiling. 'You have a great collection of photos there.'

'He's rather photogenic.' She looked down at her hands, which she clasped in front of her, and then she looked back to him.

'You look tired, Mary, and you've been on your feet for hours. Why don't you take a seat?'

'Yes, of course.' Sinking on to the sofa, she prayed that she wouldn't do anything embarrassing, like start to cry again.

Tom sat some distance from her.

Glancing at the photo album, she saw that he'd been looking at photos of Ed and Ethan, taken on a picnic one golden day in high summer when they'd driven out into the countryside in Maryland. She stared at a snapshot of Ed, caught in the midst of laughter. 'Ed knew that you are Ethan's father, Tom.'

Beside her, he jerked to rigid attention. 'Did you tell him?'

She shook her head. 'He worked it out. I think he was beginning to sense that you and I had already met—that we had some kind of past. But then, one time when Ethan visited Ed in hospital, they were having a great old chat and Ethan told him how you were able to help him because you were ambidextrous too, and, well, it didn't take Einstein to put two and two together.'

'Was he upset?'

'If he was, he didn't show it.' She groped for the handkerchief in her pocket. 'Ed was so sweet about it. He told me he couldn't think of any man he'd rather have as Ethan's father.'

'Oh, God, Mary.'

'He wanted me to tell you that.'

Tom looked as if he wanted to weep. His throat worked overtime. 'Did he—did he ask you for any details about—about us?'

'No, he avoided any awkwardness.' Her face crumpled. 'Oh, Tom, he was such a sweetheart.' Suddenly the tears were gushing down her face and the handkerchief fell from her hand.

Tom wrapped his arms around her and held her tight against his chest. His medals pressed into her as grief took hold of her and she clung to him, sobbing hard.

When at last she managed to regain control, she pulled out of his arms and saw that his eyes were red and damp too. For ages they sat together in silence, staring at the photo album, lost in their own thoughts. 'Ed was such a good man,' Mary said after some time. 'I didn't deserve him.'

'Of course you did, Mary. He kept telling me how happy you made him.'

'I tried.' She found her handkerchief and wiped her eyes, blew her nose, and after a few calming breaths she felt a little steadier. 'But anyhow... What about you, Tom? Did Colonel Maguire have anything interesting to report?'

'He spoke very highly of Ed.'

'Yes, he talked to me about Ed too. Everybody thought the world of Ed. And they've all been so kind to me.'

Tom cleared his throat. 'Maguire also wanted to brief me about a new terrorist emergency that's flared up.'

'I wondered if they were discussing something like that. Those Pentagon fellows were looking very intense.'

'Yeah.' Tom leaned forward and stared at the coffee cup and saucer on the table in front of him. He lifted them, moved the coffee cup a fraction, so that it sat more exactly in the centre of the saucer, and then set them back on the tabletop. 'Maguire wants me to do one more joint mission with the US Rangers.'

'No,' Mary whispered, fighting sudden panic. 'You can't, Tom. You told him no, didn't you?'

'No, I didn't.'

'But you can't go. Didn't you tell him you've resigned?' Impulsively, she laid an imploring hand on his arm.

'I haven't officially resigned yet,' he said, staring at her pale fingers wrapped around his forearm.

Suddenly self-conscious, Mary withdrew her hand and curled it into a tense fist on her lap, 'But you're planning to leave the Army, aren't you?'

Tom didn't answer. His dark eyebrows lowered into a frown as he studied her, as if he were trying to see deep inside her, to probe her mind, to decipher the complex secrets of her heart.

'Why does it have to be you, Tom?'

'I've been in this particular hot spot before. I was there undercover for six months last time, so I know the territory and the locals, and I'm fluent in their language.'

'But there must be other men who can do that.' The thought of Tom going back to war terrified her. 'Don't go. It sounds too dangerous.'

'It won't be any more dangerous than anything else I've done.'

'But it's *always* dangerous,' she cried.

His eyes emitted impatience. 'Mary, I've been doing this for years.'

'But that was before—'

Before I found you again—and before I fell in love with you again. Oh, dear heaven! Would Tom be shocked to know she was thinking such thoughts while she sat here in her black widow's dress? But she couldn't help herself.

He sighed. 'I shouldn't have told you about this. You're going through such a hellish rough time.'

'But that's my point, Tom. What happened to Ed could happen to you. How can you go back and take that risk?'

He sent her a quiet smile. 'I don't suppose you'd be impressed if I spouted stuff about keeping the free world safe?'

'No, not any more.' Pointing at the row of military decorations on his chest, she said, 'You've done your bit for the world.'

'Mary, believe me, I'm touched that you care.'

'You're touched?' she repeated, staring at him in puzzled horror. 'Surely you know I care? Of course I care what happens to you.' Couldn't he realise that she was petrified? If anything happened to him now, she would want to die too.

Collapsing back against the sofa, she closed her eyes. Then, as a fresh thought took hold, her eyes flashed open again. 'Perhaps I should have asked you if you have any other reasons for rushing into danger—apart from wanting to save the world.'

Tom was leaning forward with his elbows resting on his knees, hands loosely linked. He dropped his gaze to his hands.

'Is there another reason?' she persisted.

'I figure that this mission is as good a way as any to fill in time.'

Mary gaped at him. 'I don't understand. Why do you need to fill in time?'

'I've decided that I shouldn't try to move on to a new phase in my life until—until I've—sorted a few things out.'

With damp palms she smoothed her dress over her thighs. 'These things you need to sort out—do they include me?'

'Yes.'

Oh, God. Her heart began a drumroll. 'You mean you're not sure how you feel about me now?'

'I mean we both need time.'

No! She didn't need time. She could tell him right now, without hesitation, that she loved him. She'd loved him long before she met Ed, and deep in her heart she'd never stopped loving him. But of course she wouldn't tell him that.

He was right. This wasn't the time to speak of such things. No matter how she felt about Tom, she'd loved her husband too. Losing Ed had left an enormous hole in her life. She needed time to grieve and she needed every bit of leftover strength to help Ethan get through his grief.

But if only Tom didn't have to place himself in the way of more danger.

'How long will this mission take?'

'Hard to say. It's not a quick in-and-out job. There's a lot of surveillance involved and, given the complex situation, it could be close to twelve months before everything's wrapped up.'

Twelve months! Mary's legs trembled as she rose from the sofa and walked away from him, across the room to the window that overlooked her back garden. A whole year. It was a lifetime.

Four seasons. It was too long. Summer would hang around for weeks yet, and then there would be the long process of fall, while the trees gradually changed colour then lost their leaves. Winter would drag on for ever, casting its cold, dark gloom over everything. And before there was any hope of summer's return she would have to wait through spring.

Until this moment she'd always welcomed each seasonal shift, but all she could think of now was that she would have to endure twelve long months of worry and uncertainty. Twelve months for things to keep going wrong.

Twelve months of lonely silence.

As a Secret Service soldier, Tom wouldn't be able to write to her. Everything about him had to be a secret. There could never be public information released about the SAS—no photographs, no public recognition of individual achievements. Even Tom's family wouldn't know where he'd been posted.

She turned to look back at him. He stood in front of

the sofa, watching her. Dark wariness shadowed his eyes and she knew he was willing her to accept his decision.

Could she? All she wanted was to feel his arms around her again.

Was this the penance she had to pay for denying him those years of fatherhood?

Sighing deeply, she said, 'I'll be thinking of you every day.'

His eyes gleamed softly. 'Ditto.'

'Please, Tom, stay safe.'

'Yeah, sure.' To her surprise, he cracked a sudden grin. 'Don't worry, Mary. I'm bulletproof.'

How could he joke about something so serious? All she could feel was despair. He'd given her so little encouragement.

And yet...

And yet a tiny, hopeful voice inside her whispered...

In twelve months her life could take a turn towards happiness. If Tom could head off to confront danger, she would find a way to be brave for another twelve months.

CHAPTER TWELVE

As THE shopkeeper in Millaa Millaa gave Mary directions to the Pirelli plantation, his nasal drawl and easygoing manner reminded her that it had been too many years since she'd left North Queensland.

Nervous excitement sent her blood zinging as she turned her little hire car and headed out along the narrow road that wound along the crest of the range. On either side of the road green fields rolled down hilly slopes and tumbled into fast flowing rock-strewn streams.

'This part of Australia looks like America,' Ethan commented as he perched on the passenger's seat with his nose pressed against the window.

'It looks a lot like the parts of America that you're used to,' Mary agreed. 'That's because we're up in the Tablelands now, in a high rainfall area, so everything's very green here.'

Last week, when they'd visited her mother in South Australia, the countryside had been parched and dry.

Ethan watched a line of sleek black and white dairy cows making their way along a narrow trail towards a milking shed. 'I wish Tom had a cow farm instead of a tea farm. Tea's boring.'

'I'm sure there'll be some animals.'

'Do you think Tom will let me play with them?'

'We'll have to wait and see, won't we?'

As Mary said that she realised that the fields ahead on the right were cultivated with row after row of neatly pruned green shrubs. Her heart leapt. *It had to be tea.*

And then she saw the sign on the edge of the road. In green lettering on a white background—*Pirelli Tea Plantation*—and butterflies danced a giddy polka in the pit of her stomach.

Beside the sign was an open gate and a private road leading up to a large white house set into the hilltop.

Slowing the car, she turned in at the gate. The house looked rather grand. It was surrounded by beautiful terraced gardens and was two storeys high and made of white-painted bricks with a blue tiled roof. Deep verandas on both floors were flanked by dignified Roman columns.

She glanced at her watch. It was four p.m. Good timing. It wouldn't look as if she'd come expecting a meal. And it was early enough to pretend, if necessary, that she was just dropping by for a very quick call *en route* between visiting old friends in Townsville and Cairns.

Of course, a detour via the Tablelands was a bit of a stretch of credibility, but with luck Tom would be so pleased to see her that he wouldn't notice.

Just the same, she didn't feel brave enough to drive right up to the front door, so she parked her car at the bottom of the drive in the shade of a macadamia nut tree.

Holding Ethan's hand, more for her own comfort than for his, she began to walk up the drive, but with each step her nerves mounted. Was this too impertinent of her, turning up on Tom's doorstep out of the blue? She had no idea what his reaction would be. Was she completely crazy?

All she knew was she needed him. Each day without him had been misery, and as soon as the year was up she'd begun booking plane tickets and packing. And now, after a fortnight's pleasant reunion with her mother, here she was.

As they reached the foot of the steps leading to the front door she paused to admire the spectacular view. From here she could see all the way down the soft green hillside, across the pretty valley to the other side, where steep hills were covered in rainforest.

It was so quiet and peaceful here. At least it was until terrified squeals erupted nearby and a small figure in a short blue dress dashed around the side of the house.

'No, Steve, no!' the little girl shrieked. 'Stop it. I don't want to be a captured princess!'

Mary caught a fleeting impression of slim brown legs, bare feet and long dark hair as the girl flashed past them and then, hot on her heels, an older boy came chasing after her. Dressed as a pirate, with a black eye-patch and red and white spotted kerchief, he wielded a rope in one hand and a wooden cutlass in the other. 'I'm gonna lash you to the mast!' he shouted.

The girl squealed again, clearly delighted to be so terrified. Then the two disappeared, leaping from the top of a stone wall down to a terrace below.

Beside Mary, Ethan gave a gasp of excited surprise, and tugged his hand free from hers as he hurried across the grass to see where they'd got to.

'Ethan, stay here with me.'

The shouts and squeals stopped. Next minute, two dark heads popped over the wall and two dark brown pairs of eyes peered at them.

'Hello,' called the little girl, staring up at Ethan.

'Hi,' he said, smiling shyly, then looking back towards Mary.

Nimble as mountain goats, the children scrambled back up the stone wall. They were clearly brother and sister, and Mary guessed that they were Tom's nephew and niece. The girl seemed to be a little younger than Ethan and the boy a year or so older.

'Mum's at work and Nan's gone to town. No one's home except Nonna and us,' the girl said.

Mary opened her mouth, but before she could speak Ethan said, 'We've come to see Tom Pirelli.'

The girl's eyes widened. 'Hey, you talk like people on television.'

'I'm American,' Ethan said proudly.

'Wow!' The little girl smiled in open admiration. 'That's so rad. What's your name?'

'Ethan.'

'I'm Frannie and this is Steve.'

Her brother lifted his eye-patch and fingered the kerchief on his head, as if he wasn't sure that he still wanted to wear it. 'Uncle Tom's not here,' he said.

'Do you know when he'll be back?' Mary asked.

Steve shrugged. 'We haven't been told when he's coming home.'

All her happy expectation drained away. She'd been running on adrenalin for days now, and instantly she felt exhausted. This journey could well be useless. 'Do you know where Tom is?' she asked.

'Dad thinks he's somewhere in the Middle East, but Uncle Tom never tells us much about where he's going.'

Alarm spiked through her. 'You mean he's still with the Army? He hasn't come home at all?'

Both children shook their heads.

'You must have heard something. Is he all right?' She knew she sounded panicky but she couldn't help it. Tom's twelve months were up, and all she could think was that if he wasn't home he was in danger—missing in action—as Ed had been. 'Haven't you heard *any-thing*?'

'There was a call from Canberra about three months ago, but all they would tell us was that Tom was well,' said Steve.

'You'd better come inside and talk to Nonna,' said Frannie. 'She can explain. She was crying yesterday, and I heard her telling Nan that if anything's happened to Tom it's all her fault.'

'Are you looking for Mary?'

The woman hanging over the side fence peered at Tom as he stood on Mary's doorstep, his hand poised to ring the doorbell one last time.

'Yes,' he admitted.

'Are you a salesman?'

'No.' He sent another futile glance up at Mary's house. Every window was shut and the curtains were drawn. It was patently clear that no one was home, and his disappointment was so acute he wanted to let loose with a whole dictionary of swear words.

He might have done so if the nosy neighbour hadn't been there, squinting at him through fire-engine-red spectacle frames. 'Are you from the Army?' she called.

When he nodded she leaned further over the fence and beckoned. 'I can tell you where she is,' she said in a loud stage whisper.

Tom was down the front stairs and across the lawn in a nanosecond.

'She's gone back to Australia,' the woman told him, her eyes bulging with the importance of her news. 'She's taken her little boy to visit his grandmother in Adelaide. That's somewhere in the south, I think.'

'I see. Did she leave a forwarding address?'

'Not with me.' She frowned at him. 'Are you Australian too? Are you family?'

'Just—just a friend. Has she been gone long?'

'Nearly a month. If you ask me, I don't think she'll be coming back. What with losing her husband and everything, she's been so depressed this past year. She needs her mother. I told her so, and I told her she needs Vitamin B complex too.'

'Yes, well. Thank you for your help.'

He turned abruptly, clenching his teeth against his despair. *Gone back to Australia.* Why hadn't Mary waited? Didn't she know he would come to her?

Halfway down the street he reached for his cellphone and punched in the McBrides' number.

'Susan, it's Tom Pirelli,' he said when Ed's mother answered.

'Tom, how are you? Where are you calling from?'

'I'm in Arlington. I tried to visit Mary.'

'Oh, but she's gone to Australia. Didn't you know?'

'Did she leave you a phone number? Some kind of contact?'

'I'm afraid she didn't, Tom. She rang us from Adelaide, but I don't know if she's still there. Do you know her mother's address?'

'No.'

He finished the call quickly. It was useless. He didn't even know Mary's mother's married name. So much for sorting things out before he went home.

Sudden dread drenched him with cold sweat. Perhaps this was Mary's way of settling things. Was she running away from him again?

It was Nonna's birthday, and the Pirelli family were celebrating in the way they loved best. On the top terrace long trestle tables had been joined and covered with white damask cloths, and now they groaned beneath huge platters of antipasto, seafood, salad and pasta.

Farm work had stopped for the afternoon and the whole family was gathered around the long table—Nonna, Tom's parents, his brother Stefano, Stefano's wife Angela and their children—young Steve, Frannie and little Lisa.

Tom saw them all as he stepped from the taxi at the bottom of the drive. The rows of dark heads—a few streaked with grey—all familiar and dear. His family.

Here he was—home at last—and he knew that for his family, especially his mother and Nonna, it had been a hard time of fretful waiting and worry.

As he swung his kit bag over his shoulder the taxi took off with a rev of the motor and one of the dark heads turned.

'Uncle Tom!' came a sudden excited shout.

In an instant everyone was turning, jumping out of their seats. They were all shouting and cheering. Frannie and Steve were tearing down the drive to meet him. His dad was grinning and hugging his mother. Tom waved to them and his mother waved back jubilantly.

And then his heart clattered.

There were two blonde heads among the dark ones.

A woman and a boy.

His lungs compressed as if he'd free-dived to the bottom of the Pacific. His heart hurled itself against his ribcage.

Mary—her golden hair vibrant in the sunlight—was standing next to Nonna and they were hugging each other.

Now Ethan was running, chasing after the others, yell-ing a long drawn out 'T—o—m' as he tore down the drive.

How could Mary and Ethan be here, ensconced in the bosom of his family? Was he dreaming?

Rooted to the spot, Tom continued to stare at her as the children's arms circled his waist and hugged him. His heart galloped as he tore his eyes from her to the boy. Ethan was throwing his arms around him too, and with the same enthusiasm as the others.

'Let me carry your kit bag,' shouted Steve.

'No, it's too heavy.'

'We've got a new friend,' Frannie announced. 'His name's Ethan and he's from America.'

Stunned, Tom managed a choked, 'Hi, Ethan.' But his eyes were seeking Mary once more. She was still standing in exactly the same spot, with her hands pressed against her heart as she watched him.

'Your farm is neat,' Ethan shouted. 'There's a platypus in the dam.'

'A platypus? No kidding?'

The children were tugging at his arms and at his trouser legs, urging him forward, and it took a conscious effort to move. But at last they were reaching the top of the drive and he was being greeted by his mother, his father, and brother. So many hugs and back-slaps. Over their shoulders his eyes kept flashing to Mary, who stood very still on the far side of the table, tears sparkling in her eyes.

'You've been gone so long,' his mother cried. 'And there's been no word. We've been going out of our minds with worry.'

'I'm sorry, Mum,' he said, giving her another kiss and a hug. 'It was out of my control.'

Time to greet Nonna. 'Happy birthday, sweetheart. I thought I'd surprise you.'

Nonna was crying openly, which was not at all like her. 'I'm just so relieved to see you home, Toto. I would never have forgiven myself if anything had happened.'

'Of course nothing happened.'

And that left Mary.

Suddenly everyone fell silent. Or at least that was how it seemed to Tom. He felt as if the whole world had stopped. What was she doing here? His heart trembled. So did Mary's pink mouth.

'Hi, Tom,' she said.

'Hello.' His throat tightened and he swallowed.

'You see? We have a wonderful surprise too,' cried his nonna.

There was an expectant hush. Tom knew everyone was waiting for him to greet Mary. To kiss her. Her hair gleamed in the sunlight and a delicate flush coloured her cheeks. She was wearing a simple white sleeveless dress with blue flowers scattered over it and she looked as inviting as a summer holiday. But so scared she seemed unable to speak.

What was she doing here? It seemed as if the whole family had accepted her, as if they knew that Ethan...

What *did* they know? Where was his role in all this?

There were so many questions he needed to ask. But not now. Not with the family hanging on to every word.

He kissed Mary quickly, so quickly he barely felt the pressure of their lips meeting and then laughter and happy chatter broke out around them. The scene still felt like a dream. Totally surreal.

'Young Steve, run and fetch another chair,' called Tom's mother. 'I'll get another place setting. Sit down,

Tom. Sit there between Nonna and Mary and tuck in, everyone. Fausto, pour your son some wine.'

There was a flurry of rearranging place settings. A glass of wine was thrust in Tom's hand. Young Steve rushed back with a folding chair from the veranda.

'Now, let's get back to the serious business of eating,' said Tom's father. 'Tom, did you know that Mary has made Nonna's birthday cake?'

'She makes wonderful cakes,' said Angela.

His father chortled. 'I told her we should open a shop and sell tea and cake to the tourists. We can call it *Pirelli's.*'

Tom groaned softly. Sometimes facing up to his family *en masse* required almost as much courage as confronting a terrorist.

Beside him, Mary murmured, 'I hope you aren't angry that Ethan and I are here.'

'When did you get here?'

'A little over two weeks ago. I just called for a quick visit and your mother and Nonna persuaded me to stay. It's been so good for Ethan.'

He looked into her warm dark eyes, shimmering with deep emotion. 'That nonna of mine has a lot to answer for,' he said softly, so that only she could hear it.

Her fingers tensed around the stem of her glass. 'So you are angry?'

'Why have you come, Mary?'

She leaned close, and he smelled her perfume and the scent of sunlight on her clean, clear skin. 'I couldn't bear to stay away from you,' she whispered.

Something like a lightning bolt shot through him, but before he could respond his brother shouted from the other end of the table. 'Hey, Tom, tell us about your adventures.'

Unsure whether he was grateful or galled by Stefano's interruption, Tom held up his glass and smiled at his family. 'The war stories can wait. It's time to say happy birthday, Nonna. It's wonderful to be home.'

'You always look so handsome in your uniform, but enough is enough,' said his mother. 'Tell me that you're home for good this time.'

'I am definitely home to stay.'

He winked at Nonna and the old lady's eyes glowed as she smiled back at him.

Someone handed Tom a huge platter piled with fresh seafood and lemon wedges. 'I've been fantasising about food like this,' he said. 'Mary, let me serve you some. You'll have forgotten how good North Queensland seafood tastes.' Then, lowering his voice, he said, 'We'll have to talk—later.'

Much later.

The long lunch was over and Mary helped the women to clear it away. Ethan dragged Tom off to inspect the platypus that lived in the dam and when they returned the children disappeared to play hide and seek. Nonna retired to her room for a nap, Tom's father and brother hurried off to inspect a pump that had developed a sudden, mysterious leak, and the other women seemed to vanish into thin air—which left Tom and Mary alone.

At last.

And Mary felt as if she were a hot air balloon, filled with anxious hope to the point of bursting. Uneasy excitement had mounted inside her all through the long, torturous afternoon. During the meal, the slightest touch of Tom's arm against hers had sent her pulse leaping off the Richter scale.

But what was he thinking and feeling? Ever since he'd

arrived he'd been polite, friendly and charming. When he'd first seen her at lunchtime his eyes had sparked with dark, hungry heat and she'd been filled with hope, but since then he had indicated nothing. Said *nothing*.

And the relief of seeing him had been quickly overlaid by uncertainty. In Washington Tom had changed when he'd found out about Ethan. Perhaps he was still mad at her. Maybe he could never forgive her for keeping his son a secret for so many years. Perhaps he minded that she'd been so forward as to arrive here with his son, and without an invitation. Maybe he wasn't ready for her to be so decisive.

But now they were alone.

It was time to find out.

He had changed out of his army uniform into jeans and a dark brown T-shirt and he was leaning against the kitchen door frame, watching her wipe down benches that were already clean, as if her life depended on finding every last minuscule speck and crumb.

'I know my family have conveniently made themselves scarce, but how about we go for a walk?' he said.

She turned, her heart hammering, and nodded. Quickly rinsing her hands, she dried them and followed him out of the house, along the side veranda and down the front steps.

'I've discovered lots of lovely places to go for walks around here,' she said.

'Which is your favourite?'

'I like following the track from the dam around the side of the hill. It takes you to the sweetest little cottage that overlooks the whole valley. The place seems to be abandoned, but the view is even better than from here.'

His right eyebrow rose as he smiled slowly. 'Good choice. Let's go that way.'

The tracks between the tea plantings were just wide enough for them to walk side by side and Mary felt aflame from head to toe. She so longed for Tom's assurance that he was happy to see her, but the question seemed too important to ask.

'I'm so relieved you made it back safely,' she said. 'Was it bad?'

'Bad enough. It was a tough operation, but a good result. I told you I'd be fine.'

She gave an exasperated little shake of her head. 'We both know there's never any certainty.'

Tom glanced at her sharply. 'How have you been? I saw your neighbour. She seemed worried about you.'

'It's been a hard year.' *I've missed you so much.* She wondered if he had any idea how difficult it was for a woman to wait for the man she loved to return from war.

They walked on without speaking, while the afternoon shadows lengthened and a breeze whisked about her legs and played with her hair. High overhead, black cockatoos called cheekily to each other as they cruised the eastern sky with slow, easy strokes of their wings.

'I take it my family know about Ethan,' Tom said, breaking the silence at last.

Mary inhaled quickly. 'Yes—the adults know. I'm afraid your nonna took one look at Ethan and she knew everything. But the children haven't noticed, of course. It wouldn't occur to them that he was—connected to you.'

'And Ethan doesn't suspect?'

'Heavens, no. I don't think we can expect him to give up thinking of Ed as his father and, besides, he's too young to understand.'

'Yeah, that's what I figured.'

'But there will be a time in the future when he will need to know.'

He nodded.

Plucking up courage, she said, 'I hope it wasn't too much of a shock to arrive home and find us here.'

To her mortification, he didn't answer.

'Do you mind, Tom?'

They'd reached the fence line and beyond it the track wound around the side of the hill to the cottage. With his booted foot, Tom held down one strand of wire and raised the other to let Mary through. She knew he was waiting for her to step through the gap, but she stood still, waiting for his answer. 'Tom, do you mind that I came?'

His dark eyes looked so serious that they frightened her. 'It depends on why you've come.'

'But I told you. I've come because—' Oh, help, there was nothing for it but to be totally honest and thoroughly brave. 'Because I hope you can understand how much I love you. I've always loved you and I still want to marry you.'

As soon as the words were out she was swamped with terror. She ducked her head, gathered her skirt about her and scrambled through the fence. Once she was safely on the other side, Tom dropped the wire and swung his long legs easily over the top.

Beside her again, he reached for her shoulders and turned her to face him.

Her heart pumped wildly.

His eyes were dark and intense as he looked deeply into hers. 'Don't look so frightened, Mary-Mary.'

'Of course I'm frightened. You mean everything to me, Tom, and I'm afraid you can't ever forgive me for not telling you about Ethan.'

He shook his head. 'Who am I to judge? I've no idea how tough it is to be young and pregnant and to think your boyfriend's abandoned you.'

'So you're not mad at me any more?'

'I'm not mad at you.' His smile tilted sexily as he added, 'How could I be mad at you? I'm mad *about* you. Especially now that you've proposed to me so beautifully.'

Her skin flamed.

'You don't mind, then?'

'Oh, Mary, come here and let me show you how much I mind.' Pulling her to him, he framed her face with his hands and kissed her. And almost immediately the ache in her heart began to heal and she clung to him, needing his kiss more than air.

Tom, at last. Tom, binding her close with his glorious strong arms. Tom, kissing her fiercely, hungrily. Tom's heart pounding against hers.

Tom murmuring, 'Mary-Mary,' as he kissed her throat, as his hands travelled restlessly over her, chasing away all the pain of waiting—all the worry and guilt. 'I was crazy to go away for twelve months,' he groaned. 'It was too long.'

'It was torture.'

When they kissed again, it was with the knowledge that they had come full circle. This was where they belonged—in each other's arms. And it felt so good.

They teased each other, sipping and tasting and probing, growing more daring, hungry again, needing deeper, wanting more. Their embrace turned wild, losing all sense of restraint as they pressed for closer contact and their longing turned to lust. The mountain wind buffeted them as their hands became more and more possessive, their mouths more demanding.

Heaven knew what might have happened if Tom hadn't broken the kiss. Breathing raggedly, he leant his forehead against hers.

'Are you quite, quite certain you want to marry me?'

'Yes, please,' she whispered breathlessly.

'Oh, Mary.' He crushed her to him. Then, in a ragged, guttural voice he muttered, 'We've waited too long. Let's go to the cottage.' Grabbing her hand, he began to rush along the track.

'Tom, slow down. These sandals have silly heels and I can't keep up with you.'

'Then I'll carry you,' he growled, sweeping her easily into his arms.

'Put me down,' she cried, laughing. 'It's no use. The cottage is all shut up.'

Ignoring her protests, he continued on, his long strides eating up the track. He carried her as if she weighed no more than an armful of dried pasta. Another gust swept up the hillside and lifted her skirt, making it billow in their faces.

'We can't just invade the cottage,' she told him, batting at the skirt with her hands. 'We'd be trespassing.'

'Are you sure about that?'

'Yes. I made enquiries with a real estate agent.'

'Did you? Why?'

Somewhat embarrassed by her admission, she said, 'I fell in love with the cottage and I had all sorts of romantic plans for it. But there's a rotten, selfish owner who's abandoned it, but has no intention of selling.'

'Too bad.'

By now they had reached the old orchard at the back of the cottage. From the haven of Tom's arms Mary could see the rows of ancient lychee trees and, beyond them, the mangoes and avocados, and then she saw the cottage's stone chimney, its red roof and the blue tangle of morning glory flowers that climbed over the fence posts. 'We can't break in, Tom.'

He shoved the old gate open with his hip. 'Mary, I'm SAS. Break-ins are my specialty.'

'Not any more. You're a civilian now, and I can't believe you'd really break in to someone's house. Please don't.'

'Are you going to be this argumentative throughout our entire marriage?'

'Are you going to insist on breaking the law?'

Suddenly he stopped and let her feet slide to the ground. But keeping one arm around her shoulders, he nuzzled her neck. 'Sweetheart, trust me. I'm a Very Nice-a Boy.'

Laughing, she insisted, 'Very Nice-a Boys don't break the law.'

He slipped his free hand into his jeans pocket and she heard the jingle of keys as he withdrew it. Grinning, he tossed the keys in the air, caught them again, then traced the tip of a key down the curve of her neck. 'You should watch what you say about the owner of this cottage, madam. He is neither rotten nor selfish. And he is about to become your lover.'

She gasped. '*You* own this place?'

'See what an excellent coup you achieved when you convinced me to marry you? Not only do you have access to my body, but to my hearth and home too.'

'And it's such a gorgeous hearth and home,' she said, grinning wickedly.

Steering her across the veranda to the front door, he returned her smile with one that was equally wicked. 'Come inside and see for yourself.'

It was like a scene from a fairytale. The key fit the lock perfectly and the door swung noiselessly open.

'Would you like to be carried over the threshold?'

'Perhaps we'd better save something for after we're married,' she said, blushing at the implications of her words as she stepped neatly through the doorway.

Inside, she spun around excitedly. 'Tom, it's wonderful. Look at the fireplace. And the kitchen is so sweet. I love the pine cupboards and the red pegs to hang pots from.'

'Glad you like it.' He opened windows and fresh mountain air floated through the rooms. 'I bought this place some time back, when I first began to think about leaving the Army. I knew I wanted to be near the family, but I was also pretty sure I'd find it hard to adjust to living at home again.'

'It's amazing—and it's so clean.'

'Thanks to Angela. She's been keeping an eye on it for me. So, what do you think of its potential? It's very small, but we could build another floor above here, with a room for Ethan.'

'He'd adore it.'

'Do you think we'd be OK here?'

'We'd be more than OK. This is perfect, Tom. It's yours and that's all that really matters. But, honestly, I love it.'

'If we extend upwards we could add an extra bathroom and another room for the baby.'

'Which baby would that be?' she asked, suddenly coy.

'The one we're going to make,' he said, and the look he gave her sent a tide of warmth spreading through her like wine.

'Oh, Tom. I'd love another baby.'

Fingers spread, he covered her stomach with his hand.

'We'll share this little one every step of the way. I want to watch it grow inside you.'

'Yes.' Suddenly her eyes misted. 'You've missed so much. I'm sorry.'

'But we have the future.' He planted a soft kiss on her forehead and taking her by the hand, led her through another doorway. 'This is our room, Mary.'

The bedroom was surprisingly large and very simply furnished, but the view was amazing. Mary stood by the bed, with its neat white cotton throw rug covering the bare mattress, and she stared out at the sky, flecked now with flushed pink clouds, and at the valley, turning gold as the sun sank behind their hill, and she was filled with more happiness than she'd ever thought possible.

Tom stood behind her, enfolding her with his arms and drawing her back against the solid wall of his chest. He kissed the side of her neck. 'We're home, Mary-Mary.'

'Home,' she whispered. Home, for her, was Tom's arms. This cottage, this view, were delightful bonuses.

'I can't believe I have you here with me to make this place perfect,' said Tom.

'It seems too good to be true. We've waited so long.' Leaning back into him, she felt fire run beneath her skin as her bottom came into contact with the front of his jeans.

'I love you, Mary, and I promise I'm going to do everything I can to make you happy.' Lifting her hair, he kissed the back of her neck, and she arched with pleasure as his warm lips laved her skin.

Tilting her head back, she pressed kisses to the underside of his shadowy jaw. 'I love you so much, Tom. All I want is to make you happy too.'

'That can be our mission—to keep each other happy.'

'Yes.'

Their eyes met and they shared an upside-down smile, each sure that the promises they were making now were as sincere and meaningful as the ones they would make later in public when, at long last, they were married.

His hands traced sensuous pathways up her bare arms from her elbows to her shoulders, then down, and up again, and the heat and wanting inside her mounted. Impatiently, she turned in his arms and lifted her face to look directly into his eyes.

'Tom, I've never felt for anyone the way I feel about you.'

His eyes shimmered as he let the meaning in her words linger between them.

'Mary,' he murmured. 'You've always been my Mary.'

She kissed his mouth, then nuzzled his jaw. His hands gently captured her face and he returned the favour, sending kisses all over her face. Then, holding her still, he tasted her lips and teased their seam with his tongue and their kiss became hungry.

He skimmed a finger along the scooped neckline of her dress. 'This is a very pretty dress, but—'

'It has to go,' Mary whispered, her fingers flying to undo the row of tiny buttons.

'My thoughts exactly. Same with this,' he said, hauling his T-shirt over his head.

She feasted her eyes on his magnificent shoulders and the impressive breadth of his masculine chest. Unable to help herself, she pressed her face into the dark shadowing of hair on his chest, scattering kisses as she let her hands explore his smooth, satiny muscles. 'Tom, your body is even better than I remembered.'

She heard his soft chuckle and felt his hands pushing

her dress from her shoulders, unsnapping her bra and setting her a little away from him so that he could look at her.

And *look.*

'I'm afraid I've changed a bit since I've had Ethan,' she said, noticing how white and rounded and soft she appeared beside his taut darkness.

'Have you?' Reverently, he cupped her breasts. 'You're beautiful. You can only have changed for the better.' Ever so slowly, his fingers traced exquisite circles over her breasts, returning again and again to their tightening tips. Wild messages of wanton longing pulsed straight from her nipples to her loins, making her burn with readiness for Tom, wanting him to kiss her all over, to do anything he wanted. Take everything she had.

She was his for ever after.

'Have you any idea how much I want you, Mary?'

'If it's as much as I want you, I'm a happy woman.'

She wriggled her hips to free herself of the rest of her clothing and the garments slipped to the floor on a silken whisper. With similar haste Tom jettisoned his jeans.

They stood facing each other without moving, paying homage with their eyes as their desire mounted.

'Tom, do you remember the night you waited on the corner?'

'Yes, I can never forget it. I saw one brief glimpse of you at the window. And that was the last time.'

'And now you don't have to wait any longer.'

They fell into each other's arms, mouths seeking, bodies cleaving, and Tom backed towards the bed, taking Mary with him.

Together at last.

And they knew that, no matter how many times they made love in the years to come, chances were their hearts would never be quite this full, or their need greater.

This now, this love, was their reward, their long-awaited, deeply cherished prize.

If you enjoyed what you just read,
then we've got an offer you can't resist!

Take 2 bestselling love stories FREE!

Plus get a FREE surprise gift!

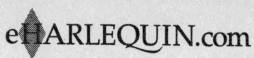